T0129410

Rebirth

War of Shadows

T Y L E R   G O L E C

iUniverse, Inc.
New York   Bloomington

iUniverse books may be ordered through booksellers or by contacting:

iUniverse
1663 Liberty Drive
Bloomington, IN 47403
www.iuniverse.com
1-800-Authors (1-800-288-4677)

Because of the dynamic nature of the Internet, any Web addresses or links contained in this book
may have changed since publication and may no longer be valid. The views expressed in this work
are solely those of the author and do not necessarily reflect the views of the publisher, and the publisher
hereby disclaims any responsibility for them.

ISBN: 978-1-4502-1920-4 (sc)
ISBN: 978-1-4502-1921-1 (ebook)

Printed in the United States of America

iUniverse rev. date: 04/02/2010

PROLOGUE

"There is a war coming."

"I have seen it as well."

Two tall figures cloaked in black robes walk together through the woods in the dark. The moon created shadows of their faces under their hoods.

"Of all the wars I have seen, I fear this may be the worst."

"And what of it—do these people have a care for us? Should we fight for them when they do not even know we exist?"

"You know who pulls the strings."

"I do."

"And you will let them."

"I cannot directly oppose them and hope to succeed."

"With the rest of us there is a chance."

"Not chance enough—we will need aid."

"How do you propose we acquire that aid? Do you propose training others? That will not go unnoticed."

"No—at least not yet—there is one strong enough who can help us."

The other paused for a second, looked at his partner, and said, "The shadow caster?"

"Exactly."

"Has one been born then?"

"No, not yet—though one lies dying as we speak."

"Dying? A shadow caster lives and I do not know? Do they?"

"Only I know—for he has yet to touch his power."

"How is that possible?"

"He will die—and that will be that. It is not him who will give us aid."

"Then hope is lost …"

"No, there is a child yet unborn—grandchild to this dying shadow caster."

"You know the chances of that child being a shadow caster. It is likely that another won't be born for several centuries."

"Chance has never had to do with the birth of a shadow caster; he is born because the times require him to be."

"Then why does one lie dying?"

"Because it was necessary for his son to feel the cold—to loathe him—so the child can be born in a proper place and live his destined life."

"Now you speak of destiny—you can't honestly tell me that after all your years you believe in that?"

"Destiny is in the mind to most, but the shadow caster is different. They will always do great and terrible things—or live the lives that will set up the future. Never has a shadow caster been absent long when great and terrible changes were happening to the world."

"And you know for certain that this unborn child will be a shadow caster."

"For certain, a shadow caster would not miss being born in this era—for man will need the extra push."

"Push toward what?"

"We will see. You can never know for certain when the darkness of man and the universe are concerned."

"What would you have me do then?"

"Nothing—not yet. You will come to me when events began to take motion. Till then, you wait."

"Yes. I will wait."

CHAPTER 1

Every thousand or so years, the world changes. It can't be stopped, it just happens. From the classical to the medieval with the spread of Christianity, then again during the Renaissance with the discovery of science, and now it is happening again.

✳ ✳ ✳

Up ... down ... Alex watched the light of the setting sun reflecting off of Hannah's quarter as she repeatedly flicked it up in the air. It was all that she had left, and Alex could boast little more. Like most people in the Americas, civil war had ripped everything away from them.

Alex was sixteen. He might be an orphan, but he wasn't sure. When he was six, his father had been fighting under the flag of the New Americans when he was separated from his mother. She had been taken off a bus by a New America force searching for traitors and spies from the Republic forces, who, at the time, controlled most the former United States.

Ten years later, he can only remember the fear. After the president was assassinated sixteen years earlier, the world fell farther and farther into chaos. The only remaining stable countries were France and Great Britain. They were the very last to leave the United Nations and were still leaning toward nondirect fighting. When there was still free press, they had been calling it World War III.

China had attempted to invade Japan but weren't able to get by Japan's newly built, state-of-the-art air force, which wreaked havoc on their battleships and carriers. Afterward, China's economy crashed because of wasting so much money on their failed invasion. North Korea then invaded northern China using new nuclear technology to level many key Chinese facilities. Russia joined in and invaded China from the northwest. The Middle East was in a heated civil war, dividing it into two nations: the Sunni and the Shia.

Alex switched his gaze from the quarter to Hannah. The setting sun reflected off of her golden brown hair, enhancing her already good features and making her appear radiant despite the shabby clothing and dirt stains. They had met about four months earlier, and Alex had been instantly taken by her. Tonight they were waiting in Boston Harbor, where they would try to buy a ride over to Great Britain with their remaining money. They had nothing left and had only two choices: join one of the thieves' gangs or the New American or Republic forces. Only one of the armies would have been possible—neither of the armies probably even wanted her—and the thieves' gang would probably make her a whore for one of its upper members. Alex had the option of joining either army or a gang, but he wouldn't force Hannah out on her own or into either of those circumstances.

She caught his gaze and smiled as she turned away. Hannah wasn't the only person traveling with him.

Alex's group consisted of nine people; they'd been working together to stay alive for about two years. Hannah was sixteen; twelve-year-old James was a great pickpocket and bread thief; Naomi and Sam were brother and sister of seven and eight. Alex couldn't recall who was which, but both carried their weight, though their bickering kept Alex and the others from sleeping many nights.

Simon was Alex's good friend from back when they still had school. Karla liked another member of their group—Mike—who was the same age as Alex. Mike could be recognized as second in command in their unofficial hierarchy, which had as much to do with size as intelligence.

Mike was Alex's superior in terms of sheer strength, but they respected Alex for getting them out of several tight jams when Mike's strength couldn't. Mike wasn't a muscle head. He was quiet and even tempered, despite his brutish appearances.

The last member of their small band was Will, their thirteen-year-old, unofficial master of knives. Alex wasn't quite sure where Will had come across all the knives, but was happy that he had. They had helped in many occasions when encountering armed merchants that were not happy with having their supplies stolen or the occasional mishap when they made had themselves too much at home on a gang lord's territory.

Alex turned his head toward the sound of a horn from a ship approaching the docks. He stood up and signaled the others to follow. He adjusted his own knife in his shirt so it wouldn't be so easily noticed. Boat captains really didn't care if they carried armed passengers anymore—unless the passengers made it quite obvious that they were armed. Mike came up next to him and kept pace for several seconds before speaking.

"Are you sure we have enough?"

"Six hundred hard-earned dollars."

Mike smiled, suppressing a laugh.

"Humph. Things have gotten cheaper, haven't they?"

"Since the oil ran out, they're forced to use hydrogen or whatever that other stuff is."

Mike smiled again, this time insecurely. He probably didn't know as much about gases as Alex did. Alex had managed to stay in school about two years longer.

"Yeah, that stuff."

"Alex?" said Simon, followed by Will. "What boat are we taking?"

Alex shrugged.

"How 'bout that one?" Will said, pointing to an out-of-commission battleship. "It looks cool."

Alex, Simon, and Mike laughed.

"What? Why can't we take that one?"

"That's a battleship, Will," Simon said.

"So? It looks cool and it would be safer than any of those unarmed transporters," Will responded.

Will had a point. There were a lot of pirates now, but there was another reason that captains didn't mind carrying armed passengers. "Will, that's what your knives are for," Alex said.

"Oh," Will said, slightly embarrassed.

"Anyway, I was thinking the freighter over there would probably be more expensive, but we could always send James to sneak cash from the well-to-do people—and it would probably be a piece of cake to steal from the kitchens," Alex said, pointing to a large freighter.

"Point," Mike agreed.

"Yeah. But what if they catch us?" Simon asked.

"Then we do what we always do when they catch us," Will said.

"But we can't kill them or run away—we'll be over water," Simon replied.

"There are always plenty of places to hide on a boat that big," Alex responded.

"I say we go for it," Mike agreed.

"Aye," said Will.

"I just ... arrh ... oh well, I guess you're right," Simon said.

Alex, Mike, Will, and Simon were the unofficial council that would make quick, simple, important decisions. That didn't mean they didn't include the others, but Naomi and Sam were too young and Karla and Hannah were often stuck behind watching when they attempted something too dangerous for them. James was too naïve to make any good decisions. The others were involved in almost every other decision-making process, but for the most part, Alex's last word was final. Alex didn't try to be a dictator—it just happened that most of what he said was right and the others trusted him.

"So what boat?" Hannah asked as she and the rest of the group caught up.

"That one," Simon said, pointing at the freighter.

"Oh, I wanted the battleship," James said, imitating it with blasting and exploding sounds.

"That's what these are for," Will said, flashing his knives. "No pirate is going to touch you while I have these."

"Oh yeah? Pirates have guns—they steal and buy them off the armies," James said.

"Then I'll do this," Will said, diving on James and starting a playful wrestling match.

Karla let out a surprised scream as the two almost hit her. "Watch out," she yelled at them.

"Come on, Karla, they're not going to hurt you—though they may hurt themselves," Mike said jokingly.

"Aw—and I assume you'll protect me," Karla said, somewhere between flirting and a taunt.

"Maybe I will," Mike said as he grabbed Karla and hefted her over his shoulder.

"Let me down," she said, laughing and hitting Mike's back.

"Does the pretty lady no longer need help?" Mike asked as he slowly brought her back over his shoulder.

"No—just not that kind," she said as they began making out, halting Mike from putting her down.

"Get a room!" Will said, getting up from his tussle with James.

Sam began dancing around his sister, singing a taunting song about Mike and Karla.

Alex glanced quickly at Hannah and saw her smile, her eyes bright. "Come on. We're gonna miss our boat," he yelled.

"No we're not," Mike said, putting Karla down.

They traveled the rest of the way to the docks without incident and only attracted a few stares from the few remaining wealthy population. Once they reached the freighter, they engaged the man standing by the entrance.

"We'd like transportation to Great Britain," Alex said.

"It'll be seventy-five for you and the big guy, seventy-five for the two ladies, and sixty for those two," he said, pointing at Simon and Will, "Oh and forty for the little guys."

The grand total came to five hundred dollars. Without question Alex handed over five hundred dollars and led the others up the ramp to the boat. Once there, a crew member handed them three sets of keys.

"These rooms are three floors down. They're not big, but we're pressed with passengers who reserved rooms so these will have to do," he said before sending them on their way.

Once they reached their rooms, they inspected them. As expected, they were all small with only two twin beds in each. The third was smaller and contained only one full-size bed. Before leaving, Karla took the key from Alex, led Mike into the room, and locked the door.

"Umm?" Alex said.

Hannah let out a small laugh, "I hope she knows what she's doing."

"I'll guess not," Simon replied. "If they keep that up, she'll be pregnant before we reach England."

"She thinks we'll be able to create stable lives once we get there," Alex responded.

"I wish I could be as sure as she is," Hannah said, stealing a quick glance at Alex.

By this time, James, Sam, and Naomi had claimed the first room.

"Great. Now we'll have them making a racket in one room and Karla will be making all those noises next door. I might as well not even try to sleep," Simon complained. They all had to laugh.

"I'll take the floor. You two can fight over the remaining bed. Hannah can have the other," Alex said as he entered their room.

"Hey, who said she got a bed?" Will complained.

Hannah turned and stuck her tongue out as she entered.

"Hey!" Will yelled as Simon ran by him to the bed. Alex hadn't expected them to take his words to heart, but he realized that he should have known better as they began rolling all over the room, making more noise than the little ones—Karla and Mike—combined.

Hannah sat on her bed cross-legged and watched Alex as he made his bed on the floor. Alex blushed as she let out a little laugh.

CHAPTER 2

"What do you think we'll find?" Hannah asked.

"What—" Alex was still mostly asleep. She was sitting on the bed with her legs stretched out, supporting herself with her arms.

"I mean in England."

"Not America?"

"I'm being serious, Alex. What do you think we'll find in England?"

In truth, Alex had spent most of his time contemplating just that.

"A job. Some peace. Hopefully stability."

"How long do you expect England to stay at peace?"

Alex truly had no idea how long Britain could stay out of the war.

"No idea."

She was slightly disappointedly.

Despite being half-asleep, Alex could pick up on it.

"What? I can't do everything—never mind stop a war."

She stared out the small circular window, and Alex joined her on the bed. The hard rain meant a long boring day on the boat. After a while, Hannah strode to the door gracefully.

Alex shrugged of his blankets and examined the rest of the room. On the other side, Simon and Will were too stubborn to surrender the bed and had separated its blankets and slept on different halves. Alex grabbed his jacket and examined his reflection in the round window. His hair was so incredibly dark brown that it appeared almost black. The grease from lack of washing added to the dark color. His face was grubby with dirt stains, but he couldn't remember not having them. His cheeks were slightly sunken and he had high cheekbones and a slight cleft chin and strong jaw line. His nose was fairly plain except for a little bump where he had broken it four years earlier. All in all, he didn't think he looked that bad for a homeless boy from Connecticut who had made his way to Boston. Grabbing his jacket, he left the room.

He went to the room where James, Sam, and Naomi had slept and knocked on the door.

"Hey, it's Alex. Any of you up?"

As expected, he heard nothing. They probably hadn't slept till exhaustion stopped them dead where they were maybe two hours ago. Next he went to Mike and Karla's door.

"You two up yet?"

"Yeah," replied Mike.

"I'm going to grab some food. Do you want some?"

"Umm …" Mike said.

"Eggs, waffles, and bacon—lots of it," Karla finished.

Alex laughed.

"Sure, meet me back in the other room. Make sure not to wake up James and the others. I think we'll need him with some energy."

"Gotcha," Mike responded.

Alex had hoped to run into Hannah before he reached the kitchen, but she wasn't there. Alex decided that the others could wait for their food a little while longer and that he should really find her. He checked most of the main rooms before he decided that she might be on the deck. *She's gonna get sick without a jacket,* he thought right before he saw her. She was soaked as she stood near the railing. Concerned, he walked toward her. When she turned, she looked as though she might have been crying. Alex's heart fluttered as he made his way toward her.

Once he reached her, he gave her his jacket.

"Thanks."

"You should—"

"I'm sorry."

"For what?"

"Earlier."

"That's—"

"No . . . I just . . . you seem to have an answer to everything and part of me believed you had an answer to this war and could—"

"Hannah, it's okay."

"No. I was being selfish. You truly are amazing. I only wish I was as strong as you," she said and began crying again. "Without you, I don't know where I would be and James Naomi and Sam would probably be lost in some gutter, if not dead."

"It's not just me."

"What? You think Mike could have done that? I'm not saying he's stupid, but he thinks more with his biceps than with his brain—and Karla's gonna suffer for that."

"That's not fair."

"Don't act stupid, Alex. Chances are if Karla and him do settle down, something in him will never forget the streets and he'll mess up big time and Karla will get dragged into it."

"That's—"

"Harsh? But it's true. I thought you were like him when we first met," Hannah said as Alex blushed. "But you're not. You tend to think before you act, but you somehow hold us all together."

Alex couldn't think of anything else to say when Hannah wrapped her arms around his neck.

"Hannah—"

"Don't talk, Alex." She kissed him for the first time. Alex kissed her back, tasting her mouth and the rain that dripped between their lips. After a while, she pulled away, smiling. Her eyes had suddenly grown wide as she noticed something behind him.

Alex turned around rapidly to see what she was looking at. A boat was barely becoming visible through the fog and rain just as Mike came out on deck.

"Thought you two were getting food, not—" He stopped to see what Alex and Hannah were looking at. "Fuck!"

The boat's intentions were clearly stated by the men rushing to the sides and how close it was coming.

"Pirates!" Alex yelled as they ran back to the entrance that led under deck.

They had almost reached it when Alex witnessed those on the other boat do the impossible. They were still nearly fifty feet off deck and nowhere near close enough to begin boarding, but they jumped the gap with what appeared to be little effort.

"Holy shit!" Mike yelled.

Alex whipped out his dagger. He heard Hannah protest as he turned to charge the closest attacker. Alex closed the distance quickly, and the man seemed surprised when Alex buried his blade into his stomach. It was weird—it was as if he hadn't even tried to avoid it or even slash at Alex with the long blade he was carrying. All the attackers were armed with an odd assortment of blades—if anything at all. Not one had a firearm.

"Alex, run!" Hannah yelled.

Others joined in on Alex's side, but few approached. Alex failed to notice that a few were dead on the deck.

"Him!" one of the pirates yelled, pointing a rapier toward Alex.

Alex grabbed the blade of the man he had just stabbed and ran for the door where Hannah stood. A pale orange bolt flew past his head. Ducking to avoid a second bolt, he felt something tug at his ankle. As he tripped, he was unable to drop his dagger and the blade in time. Hitting his head on the ground, he felt the blade on his hip. The side of his face—and where he had landed on the blade—grew warmer. Head throbbing, he realized that the blade had gashed his hip quite deeply.

"Alex!" yelled Hannah.

He felt someone grab him. He barely recognized it as Mike.

"Shit! Hannah, get out of here!" Mike yelled.

Hannah's eyes were large in fear as she ran through the doorway out of sight. The fall had taken a lot out of him and he was forced to rely mostly on Mike.

"Alex, hold on. Just need to . . . shit!" One of the attackers moved rapidly in front of them.

"Give him to me." The old man stood unarmed.

"Never," Mike yelled. A flash of light left the man's hands. Alex felt himself drop as Mike went limp. This time, he was able to brace his fall with his arm.

"Humph!" the old man said. "Take his friend as well. The girl—" Alex swore he saw the man's eyes narrow in Hannah's direction. "Never mind her."

It was all he heard before he lost consciousness.

The old man regarded the unconscious boy that lay at his feet. He swore he had seen him pass through a shield with ease, but he couldn't feel anything. *Oh well, I'll let Zanier deal with this now.*

"Tantalus, should we secure the boat?"

With Kyle injured, command had passed to Tantalus.

"What for? Pick two who can handle dragging it and let's get them back. I want to get out of the rain."

The man appeared confused and sensed no rain passed through Tantalus' shield.

"He's coming to."

A massive pain shot through Alex's head when he tried to sit up. Then all the painful memories flashed through his mind. When he opened his eyes, he saw two people in the room wearing dark-green silk robes.

"Good," said the older one as he strode to a table in the room and slipped something into his green robe. Alex realized that the younger one was a woman.

"Can I send in his friend?" she asked.

"Go ahead," the older man replied.

Alex tried to stand up again, but the pain shot through him once more.

"Oh," the woman said as she ran over to him and placed her hand on Alex's hip. She shut her eyes, and the pain disappeared instantly.

"What?"

"Magic," she said, smiling at him. "And it seems you'll learn how to use it too. Mike, you can come in now."

Alex felt a combination of excitement, awe, fear, and confusion. She left and Mike came in—they stared at each other for a while before either said anything.

"Dude, I can't believe this," Mike said.

"Wow!" Alex examined his hip but couldn't find any hint of a wound. *It really could be magic.* "What happened to …?"

"They didn't harm her. They did something to the boat and now it's following us," Mike said. "I heard them say something about checking it for more potential or something like that. They were searching for you when they boarded."

Fear ran through Alex as he realized that they probably wouldn't be too happy about him killing one of their own. "You think—"

"I think you might be a little bit important if they sent all those guys after you. Did you know anything about this?"

"No," Alex said.

"Sorry—I just had to ask."

The door opened and the older man reentered.

"You," the man said, pointing at Alex. "Come with me."

Alex stood up and followed. Mike patted him on the back as he left.

"What's your name?" the man asked.

"Alex."

"Humph—he definitely put a lot of effort in for a street rat."

"What do you mean?"

"He sent fifty men to retrieve you and it seemed they were to foolish to believe that you might just be the boy in rags standing on the deck. I think you gave Kyle what he deserved."

"Was he the one I killed?"

"Killed? Bah! None of us will die that easily—even if it was Kyle. He at least knew how to close the wound, but it must have hurt like hell."

"So I didn't kill him?"

"Nah. You just taught him never to let his guard down again when homeless kids in rags charge at him."

The insults were getting to Alex a little, but he was relieved that he hadn't killed the man.

"Where are we going?"

They entered a staircase that went up two floors.

"To see the most powerful spell caster the world has ever seen—or at least that's what we were told."

Suddenly, images of wizards and witches filled his head. Old men in outrageously big cloaks and long beards cast lightning bolts and fireballs. The older man knocked on a door and it opened by itself. The room was bigger than most on the boat. Inside, two men and the woman that had healed him were sitting around a table. Except for the table and a bed, the room was quite empty. Alex felt nervous as he recognized one of the men as the one he had stabbed. He had short, sandy-brown hair, brown eyes, and a face that was an odd mixture of round and narrow. He smiled at Alex as he recognized him. Alex smiled back awkwardly as some of the tension left him. The man in the center was probably in his late fifties with balding gray hair, but he still held on to handsome, fearsome features.

The man said, "So, this is the boy who buried his dagger into our good friend Kyle—after all the effort to track him down."

The man who had led Alex to the room laughed a little.

"Charles, you may have a seat."

The man said it so well that no one else in the room noticed the insult, but Alex saw how the man next to him was taken aback by it.

"Now tell me, boy, what is your name?"

"Uh … Alex."

The man laughed. "I mean your full name."

"Alexander Montague Savadora."

It had been a while since Alex had said his full name and it sounded weird in his mouth.

"Humph. I will not forget that name and hopefully you will give me no reason to." He was smiling now. "Now tell me, have you ever tapped into magic before?"

"I don't think so," Alex responded.

"You did when you stabbed me," Kyle said, smiling.

"Oh …"

"A subtle form of magic, but magic nonetheless," he responded.

"I think we should test him to see what form of magic he is most proficient in," the woman said.

"You're just all excited that you might have another healer because of how well he responded to your healing," Charles said.

"You have a point, Sara, but I have a few more questions," the man replied. "Sorry. It seems as though I have forgotten my manners. My name is Zanier and I'm the leader of what may be called the first magic cult in almost one thousand years."

"Oh," Alex responded.

Zanier smiled. "Zanier wasn't my birth name. That name has been forgotten to everyone—even myself. A case of amnesia. When I was twelve, my family crashed into an oil tanker. According to my rescuers, I was found in the heart of the fire with flames encircling my body—yet none touched me. They said it was a miracle, but I call it the most basic form of a shield that a mage can create." He laughed. "It seems my real gift in magic comes from my ability to create wards and shields to protect myself and others. Don't get me wrong—I am quite skilled in the other arts."

"What happened to your parents?" Alex asked.

"It's quite obvious that they died. The strain from the magic must have caused my memory to wipe out much of my life—though I still possessed most memory of stuff I had learned such as how to speak and do math. Enough of me—tell me about you."

"I might be an orphan, but I'm not sure. My dad joined the New Americans and my mom was dragged from a bus two years later by the same people my father was fighting for."

Sara looked sadly at Alex.

"That's tragic," said Kyle.

"Can you recall their names?" Zanier asked.

"My mother's was Maria, but I can't honestly recall my father's because I haven't seen him for nine years."

"War affects us all, doesn't it?" Zanier said. "We are enemies of all who fight in this World War III and aim to end it. As of right now, we are too weak, our numbers too small, and our number of skilled mages is even fewer. You see, before you are three of the best in their separate arts. I give you Kyle—the war mage master of all sorts of offensive magic and self-enhancing abilities like that large jump you saw. They focused their power inward to enhance their physical abilities and allow them to make those jumps. Next, I give you Sara—mistress of healing magic and other remedies that will do you some good. She healed your infected blade wound—one of Kyle's colleagues explained that you did that to yourself." Alex lowered his head in slight embarrassment. "And finally, Charles is a guardian—master of wards, shields, and other powerful protective fields like myself." Alex watched as each stood and bowed when they were mentioned.

Alex wondered which he would most likely fit into. He really didn't want to be a healer because the prospect of staying inside and healing the sick or injured all day seemed awfully boring—though Sara seemed nice enough. Being a war mage would be cool. Alex wanted to be able to do amazing physical feats and it sounded as if he would also learn how to do wizard spells such as shooting lightning out of his hand. If he wasn't a war mage, a guardian would be cool—he'd like being able to protect himself and others from harm.

Zanier strode over to Alex. "This won't hurt—I just need to feel the true will of your power and the way it will want to be bent." He placed his hand on Alex's head. "It won't hurt a bit—just don't resist."

Suddenly, swirls of emotions filled Alex's body. His knees buckled, but he didn't fall. He felt as though he was detached from his body. It was like being immersed in solid darkness, but this darkness was power for him to use. The supreme sense of power faded. As he returned to his normal senses, Zanier said, "Now *that* was interesting. Alex, you may leave."

"What is it?" Alex said.

"You've done nothing wrong. I just need to talk with the others," Zanier responded.

"Okay. Where do I go?" Alex asked.

"Go back the way Charles took you. From there, you and your friend can ask one of the healers to bring you to your rooms."

"Uh ... okay."

Alex left awkwardly.

"You've never had to ask us about anything before—you normally just bring us in for show and tell," said Sara.

"This is different," Zanier said.

"How so?" Kyle asked.

"His magic is different—I've never seen it before."

Charles said, "Explain."

"I'd rather show."

Closing his eyes, Zanier brought back all he had felt inside of Alex and sent it mentally to the others. Opening his eyes, he turned and asked, "What do you think?"

It took a while before they responded. Kyle was the first to speak. "It was all dark, but I could tell it was there because of the absolute power of it."

Sara said, "Kyle has a point and I think I've found why he was so easily healed. His adaptive power is willing to accept helpful energy and capable of transforming itself so it can resist harmful energies. I believe it could be used to avoid the protections of others."

Zanier had sensed the same thing, but he hadn't expected any of them to pick up on it so fast.

"Good—you've gotten better."

"So you mean?" Charles asked

"Yes. When Alex is trained, I believe our shields will be useless."

"So what is he?" Kyle asked.

"A wielder of shadows—a magician of darkness. I've read of them and their powers. I believe he is a gift to our cause—as well as its possible undoing," Zanier explained.

"What do you mean?" Sara asked.

"If the books can be believed, shadow magic is volatile and difficult to control. Oftentimes it has a will of its own and has been known to take control of its wielder."

"Is he powerful?" Charles asked.

All Zanier could do was smile at him.

Alex moved briskly down the corridor to the healer's room. He was excited about his meeting with Zanier, but was still in shock. He wished that he could have told him what type of magic he was going to learn how to use—or if they were not hostile, when he could see his friends again.

He knocked at the door to the healer's room. A woman and a young man opened the door.

"Hey, Alex," Mike said. "What did they tell you?"

"Not much. Let's go—I'll tell you more." Turning to one of the healers, he said, "Zanier wants one of you to show us to the rooms we'll be staying in."

"Oh … follow me," the woman said. "Did he tell you what magic you would be using?"

"No. Why?"

"Normally … well it doesn't matter. He does strange stuff."

She led Alex and Mike farther down the ship. Alex counted two levels before she stopped at a door. She tapped the handle before opening it and said good-bye to Alex before leaving.

"So—what happened?" Mike asked.

"Zanier is their leader—he's different."

As he explained to his friends, Alex tried to focus on his feelings.

Alex felt something inside and recognized the power he felt earlier with Zanier. Focusing wholly on it, he didn't notice Mike's amazed stare and his slow steps back. He could hear yelling from outside his door, but he ignored it. There was nothing more important right now than bringing his power out. Everything around him vanished from Alex's conscious thoughts. The power flooding through him made him feel more alive than he ever had.

"Alex?" Mike asked timidly.

His hands were shrouded with darkness, the room had dimmed, and the floor contained a dark mist.

"Open the door!"

There was yelling coming from the outside. Finally, there was a flash. The door flew open and two men came in. Alex recognized one as Kyle.

"Alex, what do you think you're doing?" Kyle turned to the mist on floor.

A flash shot from his hand to the floor. A surge of rebellious anger shot through Alex. As he pointed his hand at Kyle, it slammed a cone of dark energy into Kyle and the other man.

Surprised, Alex took a step back. Kyle fell to his knees while the other man collapsed unconscious against the other wall.

"Alex, what did you do?"

Kyle was struggling to breathe while attempting to stand up. Alex felt something flare up around Kyle. Alex guessed that it was a shield.

"I—," Alex said, staring at his darkness-covered hands.

"Damn it! Control yourself," Kyle said with a strained voice.

Zanier entered the room and said, "Alex, I see you've released your power. I believe it was a mistake not to inform you about what you can do."

Taking a few breaths, he said, "You're a shadow magician or shadow caster—master of the dark energies and shadows of the world. I believe now is an appropriate time for a control lesson."

He strode calmly over to Alex and said, "Focus on returning your powers back to where you brought them from."

Alex focused on them, but felt a massive resistance that hadn't been there when he brought them out.

"As I thought. It seems that everything will be backward for you. Normally novices feel a resistance when releasing their powers. It seems for you it'll be quite the opposite."

He grabbed Alex on the forehead. Instantly, Alex's hand shot up and grabbed Zanier's wrist. Alex hadn't meant to do that, but he couldn't release his grip.

Zanier's face strained with focus, Alex could feel all his power shooting through his hand into Zanier's wrist. There seemed to be something blocking its path. Trying with everything he had, he still couldn't stop. He could feel Zanier aiding to his resistance effort. Alex felt his grip loosen before everything went black.

CHAPTER 3

Alex leaned on the railing on the rear of the boat and looked down at its wake. His stomach turned in a combination of seasickness and apprehension. He had just been released from the medical floor after having to endure Sara's teasing. She had joked about him being the only person that she had to heal twice in one day. He had been unconscious while she had healed him. Alex could still feel the splitting headache that she claimed to have greatly weakened.

The fog had thinned and the rain had stopped, but the day still remained miserable. Alex guessed that it was nearing six, which his stomach confirmed as he realized he hadn't eaten all day. Hearing footsteps, he saw Mike approaching. To Alex's dismay, he noticed that Mike walked a little more carefully and made sure he had at least five feet between them. He was carrying two trays with sandwiches—one was half eaten. Making sure not to breach the five-foot barrier, he handed a tray to Alex.

"Want some?" Mike slurred through his full mouth.

"Sure."

Alex was slightly taken aback by his friend's precautions, but realized it was expected after what had happened.

"You think they'll let us back across?"

Alex turned his gaze to the second boat. It was held in tow about three hundred yards away and Alex assumed that it was some form of magic.

"Dunno."

"Dude—that was some crazy shit you did."

He remembered the feeling when he had drawn his magic, but then remembered how he had lost control of it. Sara had explained that he had drained all of his energy on Zanier, which had allowed him to regain control. The amount of energy he released would have been enough to kill any other mage—and it had taken about five healers and several other spell casters to drain the energy from Zanier. She also said that the whole thing was made harder by not being able to actually feel it. Zanier couldn't do it himself since his focus had been on keeping the energy away from vital areas.

"I almost killed them."

"I half expected you to blast me," Mike said, breaching the five-foot barrier and patting Alex on the back. "You didn't—don't feel bad. You just need to learn control, that's all. I heard one of those wizard guys talking about it. He also sent me to get you—the food was my idea."

Alex smiled. *At least someone's happy.* Alex wanted to learn to use his powers more than ever—not only because of the power he would have, but also so that he didn't blow someone up if he accidentally brought his powers out again.

He followed Mike who was already five steps ahead of him.

✳   ✳   ✳

Kyle paced nervously, looking up only when he was about to walk into one of the foot-thick steel walls in the massive dueling area in the center of the boat. Zanier seemed amused by his apprehension.

"Why do I have to teach him?" Kyle asked.

"I'm too weak right now and you're most equated with his powers."

"Yeah. He broke my shield, stabbed me, and blasted me with his shadow energy."

"My point."

"He's powerful and has no control. What am I supposed to do if all hell breaks loose like last time?"

"Then you shield it or counter it—and don't have him take it all out at once. Plus he's worn down and you've yet to use any magic."

"Well, I did if you count that useless shield."

"Make a stronger one."

Kyle gave Zanier a dirty look as he continued to smile.

"I think I'll just blast away if he loses control," Zanier laughed.

The sound of footsteps caught his attention. The door swung open heavily, revealing Alex and his friend.

"Well, here goes nothing," Kyle said to Zanier, which only served to make his smile even wider.

Alex entered a large room with the type of ceiling that he hadn't expected in a boat. Kyle was standing in the center of the room and Zanier was standing slightly off to his left.

"Hello again, Alex," said Zanier. "Now I believe is a proper time to continue your control lesson."

He paused as Alex continued walking in.

"Good luck," Mike whispered in his ear before leaving out the back.

Zanier continued to speak. "Kyle will be your instructor. You did a good job in draining much of my energy while Kyle here only managed to get stabbed and blasted so he hasn't used much of his power."

Alex noticed the embarrassment on Kyle's face.

Kyle said, "According to Zanier, your power will be much harder to control than release, which is normally the opposite with the main three disciplines. Try taking your power out again, but this time, stay in control and only take a little."

Alex focused. Unlike the last time, his power didn't feel so powerful or as if there was less energy in it for him to draw on. Alex carefully tried to focus on a small bit of his power.

"Try to make your power do something—doesn't matter what—but make sure you can control it the entire time."

Following Kyle's advice, he tried to make his energy visible, wrapping it around his right hand. A faint dark aura surrounded it and he could hardly make out his hand inside it.

"Good."

Astonished by what he had done to his hand, he decided to cover his entire body. Focusing on his energy again, he brought enough out to cover himself.

"Alex, what are you doing?" Kyle asked.

Alex noticed Zanier smiling.

"Can you see me?" Alex asked.

"Hardly—what are you doing?"

Not satisfied by Kyle's answer, he focused on more of his energy. Intensifying the shadows around him, he tried to shape them so they would grow fainter.

"Alex!" Kyle yelled.

"It seems our shadow magician has figured out how to nearly turn himself invisible," Zanier said. "I'm curious."

Zanier reached up with one hand toward the large light on the top of the dome and the room grew darker. Smiling at Alex, he said, "Just what I thought."

Alex smiled as he looked himself over. He was completely invisible.

CHAPTER 4

Alex ran up the stairs in search of Mike. Zanier had said something about not wanting him to become too tired. He was excited about what he had done and wanted to tell Mike about it. He flew around the last flight and onto Mike's floor. He rounded the corner and almost took out a pale woman. He knocked vigorously on Mike's door when he noticed that the key was in the lock. Confused, he opened the door.

"Mike?"

No answer. The room was empty.

"He left."

Alex spun around and faced Sara. "He wanted to go back to the other boat so Zanier had one of the war mages carry him over," she said softly.

"Oh," Alex said, feeling let down. "Can I go back?"

"No, I'm sorry. Zanier wants to keep you here."

"Why can't I just come back when he wants me to train?"

"I don't know, but you can ask him tomorrow. He'll expect you to be in top form. From what I hear, you're going to be training pretty hard."

Alex fell on one of the empty cots and tried to sleep. He had no idea what time it was, but he knew that his body—

as well as something else quite hard to explain—wanted to sleep. He tried but couldn't fall asleep because he kept thinking about his friends—and he really wanted to see Hannah. He could still feel her arms around his neck and her lips on his.

✳ ✳ ✳

As Mike entered the room, Karla was on her feet and in his arms in just seconds. Hannah desperately looked around, hoping to see Alex enter behind Mike.

"Where's Alex?" Hannah asked.

"He's still on the other boat."

"Why? These mages have been all over the boat, randomly checking people for something. Mike, what's going on? What do they want with Alex?"

"I think they said they're looking for talent."

"Talent?" Simon said, entering the room with Will.

"People who can be trained to be mages like them," Mike answered.

"What do they want with Alex though? Is he … one of them?" Hannah asked.

Mike said, "Well, yes—but he's different. He's a shadow mage—I think that's what it was called."

"What's that?" Will asked.

"He does stuff with shadows and darkness. He … it's kinda scary. When I left, he couldn't really control it that well," Mike said. His eyes appeared to have lost focus.

"What do you mean?" Hannah asked softly.

"He came back to the room and he was off. They showed him something about his power. By the look on his face, it was as if he wasn't in control of his own body. I think Zanier is their leader."

"Did he attack you?" Karla asked.

"No, but if it wasn't for that older mage, I don't know what Alex would have done."

"Alex wouldn't ever—" Hannah said.

"That wasn't Alex attacking them—it was his powers. I don't know what something like that could do," Mike said.

"Do you think they'll check us—I want to be able to use magic," Will said. "That would be sweet."

Hannah smiled at Will. He was always good at lightening the mood. Mike smacked him in the back of the head.

"Ouch! What was that for?" Will said, completely surprised by Mike's reaction. Simon put his hand on Will's head and ruffled his hair. Simon was positively put out. "All right. I'm not six years old—I know what's going on and I just said that it would be sweet to use magic!"

"Well, chances are good that they're going to check this entire boat before they are done," Mike said. "I guess I can't use it. Otherwise, I can't see why they would have let me come back. I think they're going to train Alex really hard."

"Oh," said Hannah. "You think they'll let us across to see him?"

"I doubt it," Mike said. "When I saw you two on the—"

"I forgot a jacket—he brought me his," she replied.

Mike was confused for a second before he caught on.

"Oh—okay."

"Do you know where they're taking us?" Hannah asked.

Mike shrugged, "I have no idea."

"So—what do we do?" Will asked.

"Wait for now, I guess," Mike said. "Nothing we can do till we get closer to land."

❄ ❄ ❄

Left and right, Alex dodged Kyle's attacks. Zanier definitely wanted him to be in top form. He hardly let Alex rest, constantly training him in more than just magic. It had been a week since he had discovered his powers and he had hardly rested. Zanier would send for him at the crack of dawn and make him run four laps around the boat. After that, he would eat a short breakfast and be sent off with Charles where he'd practice "control." Charles would have him send a pulse of power toward him as he stood protected in one of his shields. Throughout the week, Alex's attacks—and his confidence—had slowly grown more powerful. Charles spent the hour before lunch explaining how to use his powers to protect himself. After lunch came the most challenging part. His lessons with Kyle took place in the big dome room. Kyle would set up an obstacle course in which Alex would have to get through and touch Kyle. While this was going on, Kyle was lobbing weak attacks at Alex called stun blasts. They started taking their toll after three to four hits. After six or seven, he could hardly get over the four-foot wooden barrier at the end. Alex was about halfway through the course and had yet to be hit. He still had to walk across a thin fifteen-foot beam and had no cover. Kyle, taking advantage of this, was sending attacks at Alex one after another. Alex quickly deflected one when he realized he wasn't going to dodge it. When it dissipated harmlessly off his shield, he made a move he had never done before. Kyle wasn't expecting Alex send out two quick bursts of shadow energy. Kyle deflected one, but hadn't seen the second and it struck him full in the chest. It only stunned him for the split second. That was all that Alex needed and he quickly darted across the beam and dived through the tire. By the time he was through the tire, Kyle had recovered and sent a stronger stun blast at Alex.

Realizing this, he raised his shield. As it struck, Alex could feel the blast draining him slightly. He quickly dove behind a wooden wall.

With his back to the wall, he looked at the next obstacles. About ten feet away was another wooden wall and a series of short wooden poles. All he could see after that was the traditional wooden barrier at the end. Relieved, Alex took a deep breath.

The private lessons with Zanier came back to him. He had figured out how to sense other people like radar. He could send out pulses of energy that would pick up on living creatures—better on those that could use magic—in however big an area Alex wished. It also allowed him to sense surface emotions. That—and perfecting his "stealth mode"—had been all he had done. He was able to turn invisible in the dark and become immune to all sorts of motion- and sound-detecting devices. This room was far too bright to turn invisible. He had tried to darken the light, but it was protected by barriers that he couldn't get through. He had a feeling that Zanier was behind it.

Alex reached out to sense what Kyle was feeling, but only got irritation. He ran to the next wall and felt a stun bolt go flying over. Next he had the pools. There was one other trick that Alex had discovered on his own. He could replace the exhaustion of his own physical energy with his shadow energy and could even increase his physical performance by the strength and amount of shadow energy he used. Infusing his legs with energy, he flew across the first three poles. Kyle had bided his time and a particularly powerful and well-aimed stun bolt headed straight at Alex. Unable to maneuver on the wooden poles, he had to raise a shield. The blast struck and Alex could feel the slight drain of his powers. It annoyed him how shielding himself seemed to take more out of him than other mages. Even Kyle—who was known to be particularly bad at shielding himself—seemed to hardly flinch when he shielded himself against Alex's blasts. Alex jumped to the fourth one—glad he hadn't dropped his shield—as a quick blast from Kyle struck. Quickly Alex jumped to the fifth and sixth and was about to jump on the seventh when Kyle sent a low blast at the pole itself. Unable to fix his trajectory, he stumbled and fell flat on his face, biting his lip. Alex tried to stand as he tasted blood and became quite aware of the growing warmth on his forehead. Alex felt a burst of pain on his right side as he was lifted off the ground and thrown five feet.

By this point, Alex had no sense of direction. Between the throbbing pain in his forehead and the steady flow of blood, he could hardly see or focus on anything. Trying hard to focus, he knew he needed to stop Kyle for half a second or things were going to get worse. Focusing his energy, he released a giant blast that radiated from his body. Quickly realizing exactly how powerful the blast had been, he tried to find his final obstacle, but realized that it had been grotesquely warped.

"Alex! What was that?" Kyle said furiously. "Are you trying kill us?"

"I … I couldn't see—" Alex gave up trying to stand up and fell back.

"So you release your power in a huge dome."

"Uh—"

"I thought Charles was teaching you how to control your blasts?" Judging by the sound of his voice and his pacing, Kyle was quite distraught. "I told Zanier that leaving offensive magic training to a guardian was a bad idea."

"What did I do?" Alex was quite curious at the damage he had done.

"Can't you see? Look around!" Though Alex couldn't see Kyle's face, he assumed that he must have been looking at him as if he was some kind of idiot.

"I told you I can't see."

Kyle must have noticed the mess that was Alex's forehead. "Uh, wow. I guess I need to get you to the healers."

"That would be nice."

Alex tried to smile, but only managed to spit out some blood. He was feeling light-headed and hardly noticed Kyle picking him up.

✳ ✳ ✳

"My God, Kyle! What did you do to him?"

"I was training him," Kyle said.

"More like you used his head as target practice."

"He fell. Anyways, you should see what he did to the training room."

"Sara's here. You can show me the training room."

Alex heard two sets of footsteps leaving and another set entering.

"By God, I can't wait till I get my hands on him," said Sara.

Alex could feel the same warm sensation from healing on his forehead that had become quite familiar during his first day with the mages. The sensation calmed his mind and he felt himself drifting toward unconsciousness.

✳ ✳ ✳

Zanier paced inside his room. *There was a mistake—somewhere there was a mistake.* He had gotten word about what Alex had done and felt nothing. It had been chance that Kyle and the other mage had seen shadows seeping out of Alex's room and called Zanier, but it had been a small amount of power. It had surprised him when he felt nothing during their other training lessons, but he must have felt this. After Alex's blast, he had ordered immediate repairs to the dome due to its location on the boat and the safety of those aboard, but that was the least of his problems. How had they been able to sense Alex from so far away? Tantalus had been able to point straight at him from five miles away without help from other mages, but on his own boat he couldn't feel him at all. He hadn't talked to Tantalus about it, but he figured that they both felt the same way. Tantalus had been acting odd since then. *No, we couldn't make that mistake. The chance of two spell casters on one boat were so slim and they had sensed that power right where Alex was and on the deck. There was only that girl—could she have been the one that Tantalus had felt?*

Sara had been fairly silent on the walk back to the training room. She hadn't seen the room yet, and from what Alex had heard, the damage was many times more than what he had planned.

Sara cleared her throat. "Zanier ordered immediate repairs on this room. He also wants to see you after you've seen what you've done."

Alex impatiently went through the short hallway to the room. Debris was everywhere—unrecognizable material was bent and distorted. Wood bent as if it was metal melted in extreme heat. Unknown material in exotic shapes was the least of it—the entire dome of the training area had uneven ripples throughout it.

"What did I do?"

Sara looked dumbstruck. "I think that's why Zanier wants you."

"Okay."

Alex expected Sara to follow him, but she went deeper in the room and was talking with the man in charge of the repairs. Alex headed toward Zanier's room alone. The boat that he had managed to get lost on the first few days was now familiar to him. Zanier's rooms were located on the first floor below deck—though that was not the room that he favored. He spent most of his time in his study, which had once been the control room. It would have been where the captain controlled the boat, but Alex quickly realized that this boat didn't run or steer as any normal boat did.

Skipping over the floor where Zanier's room was, Alex made his way to the study. Alex's assumption was right and the door opened before he could knock twice. Zanier faced out the large window to the front deck and the sky was now streaked with the reds, oranges, and yellows of sunset. Judging from the sun's location, he figured that they were headed south. Judging by the sporadically placed mess of books on his desk, Alex deduced that Zanier had done some frantic reading. Zanier motioned to the seat in front of his desk as Zanier sat in his own.

"Do you know what you did?" Zanier's tone was calm, but something about his eyes made Alex uneasy.

"Not really. It looked all messed up and things were warped—"

"Warped! You somehow warped the matter of the objects in that room. Do you know how you did that?"

"Umm ... I was trying to strike Kyle, but because my forehead was bleeding, I couldn't see well. I just tried to send my energy out in a wide area."

Alex thought about his response as Zanier continued to watch him. *What did I do?*

"It seems you are more powerful than I thought." He flipped a page in the book in front of him. "It says here that those who wield the shadows can also manipulate the shadows of objects which directly shift the matter—changing its shape or moving it to another place. Do you know what this means?"

"I can warp stuff by changing the shape of its shadow?"

"Exactly! I'm going to ask you to do something for me in a few days, but I would like you to master this new ability until then."

Alex was shocked. "What do you want me to do?"

"I will tell you later." Zanier motioned to the door and Alex heard a faint click as it was locked. "I don't want anyone intruding on this."

Zanier put an old mirror on the desk and positioned it so it left a nice shadow. "What do you want me to do?"

"Bend the shadow"

"How?"

Zanier only smiled, sitting back in his chair and taking care not to block the fading sunlight.

Exhorting his will, Alex stretched it out toward the shadow of the mirror. He felt his control flicker as he touched the shadow and felt himself thrown back to his own mind. Alex blushed as he realized Zanier's smile was bigger. He wasn't exactly a master of stretching out his will. He had spent most of his training on strikes and defenses. This didn't require him to stretch out his will to anything but his own power. He regained focus and tried it again—even more carefully than before. He braced himself as he entered the shadow and realized what had shot him back. The shadow seemed to contain its own supply of power—similar to, but not as extensive as, his own. Alex tried to focus on the edges as if it was his own power. He was gratified to see the corner of the mirror move like a dense liquid, swelling and bending as Alex used his power on it.

"That's enough."

Alex quickly snapped back to reality and stared at the malformed glass. He realized exactly how much it had taken out of him and he fell back against his chair.

"Tomorrow morning, you will meet me here and we will continue working on this little trick. Till then, good night." He motioned his hand toward the door; it unlocked and opened.

Alex remembered a question that he wanted to ask. "Could I head over to the other boat to see my friends soon?"

"When you can get yourself there."

"Why can't someone else get me across?"

"Consider it motivation."

Zanier started to close the door and Alex had to jump backward in order not to get hit.

Perplexed by Zanier's behavior, he went back to his room. For the first time since he started his training, he felt empty. It had taken so much of his time that he never really got to miss his friends. He thought of Hannah's kiss again and how the moment had ultimately landed him here. He wanted to see them again—but how? He focused his power on his shadow and willed it to move. To his surprise, it vanished and instantly appeared a foot to the right in another shadow that went across his desk. It had been shrouded in dark energy, but there it was in one piece. Alex went over and grabbed it—he finally knew how he would get across to the other boat.

CHAPTER 5

As usual, Will was awake before everyone else. He stared at the boat that somehow kept them in tow. Alex was somewhere on that boat. Will had never truly appreciated what Alex had been able to do for all these years. No one really knew what to do on the boat. James had grown bored of pickpocketing and exploring the boat. Mike and Karla were never seen more than six inches away from each other—if they were seen at all—since the mages had brought the news that Alex could use this cool type of magic. Naomi and Sam had officially driven Simon insane after a week of being the only one keeping them under control. Since Hannah had been abnormally quiet—which was saying a lot since she was naturally silent—something must have happened right before they took Alex. She had been extremely relieved when Mike came back with news that they weren't going to harm him and were, in fact, going to train him. Hearing footsteps behind him, Will lifted himself in his chair.

"Hey," said Hannah.

Will stretched and said, "Hey."

"When do you think he'll come back?" She was staring longingly at the other boat.

"No idea. According to Mike, he almost killed himself and two other mages by accident. They probably need to make sure he doesn't do that again."

Wrong answer. Something shifted in Hannah's expression and she turned away quickly. Will had never seen Hannah cry and it was slightly disturbing to him. She had always been so strong. Will thought of how Alex's presence made them all stronger. He knew that he had meant something more—and Hannah was suffering the most in his absence.

He put an arm around her to comfort her, but she was determined not to let anyone see her like this. She wiped her eyes and ran back down the deck of the boat. Confused, Will grabbed a knife out of his arsenal and began fiddling with it.

✳   ✳   ✳

Zanier stood upon the rear of the boat and could make out a boy fiddling with a knife on the other boat. However, that wasn't of interest to him—it was the girl who had just run down the deck.

Charles walked up to his side with another mage right behind him. "You think we grabbed the wrong person?"

"Think? I know I can't sense Alex's power from two feet away. We found him by chance."

"So who is it?"

"That girl. When we attacked the boat, she had her arms around him. They were kissing I think—being that close, we assumed it was Alex since he avoided Kyle's shield."

"So when do you want me to get her?"

"I'm going to have a talk with Alex—there is something I need him to do. Alex is going to do something for us. During his absence, we are going to train that girl. We must make sure she's loyal to us. Something about Alex's presence can be sort of commanding and I think his friends are quite loyal to him. I also don't know how long we can control him. He's trying stuff too quickly and progressing to fast. He's subdued now, but I can already see his increased confidence. Soon I think he might be willing to even oppose us—if we give him any reason to."

"All right. I'll get her now. What is Alex going to be doing?"

Zanier smiled to savor the moment. "Robbing Fort Knox."

Hearing this, a smile crossed Charles' face.

* * *

Still stiff from sleep, Alex knocked on Zanier's study. In his daze, he didn't notice the steps behind him.

"That won't do you any good when I'm out here," Zanier said, nearly sending his head into the precariously low lamp over the study door. "Good morning, Alex."

"Good morning, Zanier," Alex said, no longer in a dazed stupor.

"Good. You brought the mirror. I will be teaching you several very important skills today—though I'd rather you had more time to learn them."

"Why not?" Alex was confused about why they were short on time. "Are we going someplace?"

"You will be, but you will need to learn these two skills before you leave. Flight and teleportation are two abilities you can learn, according to my text, as by those who wield darkness."

"Oh, I think I learned teleportation last night."

Alex was suddenly incredibly excited; he hadn't tried to move himself, but he thought he could do it with some practice. Learning to fly would be sweet. If he learned how to do those two things, he would be able to finally get to the other boat and could finally see his friends and Hannah again. "Let's start."

Zanier said, "Good. That'll help and flight is fairly simple. Any caster can do it if they possess significant strength. It seems that the same principle is used for you as for us." Zanier opened the door to his study and Alex followed him in.

He closed his eyes and Alex felt pulses from beneath him. With that, Zanier rose off the ground. "The reason you don't see us flying around is that this is an incredible waste of energy and can make you feel as if you just went all out in a magic duel to fly half a mile. Teleportation is impossible for us, but not for you." He landed softly on the ground. "From what I read, teleportation—in comparison to your flight—is many times more power consuming and, unlike flying, it has some requirements before you can actually do it. You must stand in a shadow to begin with and end in a shadow, but it says that shadow mages like you can do it much easier at night—not needing a shadow as a start or end place since darkness is everywhere."

"What do I have to do?"

"For flying, it's as simple as focusing on your power. Exert it underneath you—not like a blast—as if it were air rushing out of your legs toward the ground."

Alex had done a ton of blasts and knew how to exert power, but he decided that the closest thing to what Zanier said was to rush focused amounts of power out underneath him. Nothing could have prepared him for the rush of air and darkness that lashed underneath him—it was nowhere near as peaceful as Zanier's flight. Pages flipped in books—some flipped over—and the loose paper on Zanier's desk flew out the window. In the middle of Alex's little windstorm, he raised off the ground and abruptly stopped before the ceiling. He crashed to the ground, losing his balance and falling promptly on his butt.

Alex expected a smile at his clumsiness or disgust at messing up the room even more than it was, but Zanier was deep in concentration.

"What did I do?"

"Nothing—onto teleportation," Zanier said with subtle hint of anger.

* * *

Charles hated wearing robes in front of people outside the boat, but Zanier said that it was necessary. Looking impressive and different would help influence them. He made his way down the halls of the boat, wary of every stare. He scratched nervously at the growth under his chin. Charles never understood why he got nervous just before he had to do any type of speaking to complete strangers—particularly to large numbers of them—because he was really good at it. *Better than being cocky and messing up everything,* he thought as he knocked on the door.

"Hello?"

An attractive tan girl with dark hair answered the door, but it wasn't who he was looking for.

"Is there another girl in here? I believe her name is … Hannah," Charles said with genuine kindness and softness.

The girl frowned for a second and said, "Why?"

Charles knew that she was going to be irritating—there was absolutely no trust in her voice. Charles smiled to himself. *Good instincts—let's hope this Hannah is a bit less observant.*

"I have something important to tell her directly from Zanier—the head of all mages," he said with a slight bow. He never hesitated to resort to flattery—especially subtle kinds.

The girl backed away from the door, opening it the rest of the way. Charles realized from her posture that she had given in more out of her realizing that he was coming in no matter what than any persuasive argument. Anyway, he could care less why it worked—as long as it did.

"Umm … come in. Hannah?" she said, turning to another girl sitting on the floor with two much younger individuals. She was coaxing them to eat something green from their plates. "He wants to talk to you."

When Hannah stood beside the first girl, Charles instantly began contrasting them. They were the same height, but Hannah looked taller due to her slenderness and the suppleness of her body. The other girl was curvier and slightly heavier—or at least appeared heavier because of her expansive bust and curves that Charles so clearly noticed. Had he not been under Zanier's strict orders, he may have tried to see how good he was at persuasion with this one—even if she was not quite eighteen. However, Charles was unnerved by the vast well of power beyond Hannah's eyes.

"Well, well. Zanier was not mistaken—it's not every mage whose power can be felt by looking into one's eyes," Charles said.

Hannah's gaze grew wider and the power flickered as if it had been stroked. Whether it was pleasure or pain, he could not tell.

"Me?"

Charles smiled kindly and bobbed his head in friendly laugh. "Yes, you. We thought it was Alex, but it seems we were mistaken. Alex is gifted and powerful, but with a rather different type of magic. We found him by chance—it was *you* that we've been searching for."

"What? How?"

Charles deliberately misinterpreted her vague question. "You two were in rather close contact before we boarded. It was easy to miscalculate and assume that it was him since he stabbed Kyle—and especially since your power was rather enveloping him," he said.

Hannah's fair skin flushed and the other girl's mouth opened wide. Apparently, Hannah had told her nothing.

"What were you two doing?" the other girl asked, somewhere between surprise and a friendly taunt.

"Umm ... nothing, I was just ... umm ... telling him how ..."

"How wonderful he was with your arms around him and your lips on his!" she said as Hannah turned even redder.

"We only kissed. We only ... well, I want ... but ... he was so nice ..." Hannah was completely flustered. Charles decided it was a good time to speak—especially while her mind was on Alex.

Charles cleared his throat to interrupt. "I'm sorry, but we don't have that much time—and you might have time to catch Alex before—"

Charles stopped in surprise as Hannah grabbed her belongings and rushed out the door. "So long to you, miss," he said with an exaggerated bow and a smile of relief.

✳   ✳   ✳

Karla had been startled by the mage and unnerved by the smile he let slip before he closed the door. She sighed and put her hands on her hips as she fell onto the bed behind her. She turned to where the two little ones had been eating and realized that they had disappeared. She closed her eyes and let out another sigh in exasperation. Alex never said anything, but made no secret about his views on how often her and Mike did it. If Alex was worried about her being a mom—she was basically already one in terms of looking after Naomi, Sam, and James—at least it would be hers. At this, her hands gravitated to her belly. She opened her eyes and left the room to find Naomi, Sam, and James.

※　※　※

Zanier had abruptly ended the lesson that Alex thought would have taken forever. He was forced to travel from one shadow to another by opening a void between two points and focusing all of his essence on the other spot.

Alex hurried to follow Zanier down the hall. Though Alex was younger, Zanier was several inches—and a sizable number of pounds of muscle—Alex's superior and moved quickly for his age, making it difficult for Alex to keep up as they strode to the dock.

"There—see the shadow on the other boat. Picture yourself there and, with all your will, picture your power there and you will get there."

Alex shrugged to himself, hearing Zanier repeat the instructions he had given him for the past hour. "When you come back over, you'll find a man waiting for you. He will tell you where you're going and what to do there—plus he'll give you some gear to make it easier on you."

Alex, shocked at his behavior, couldn't even ask a question. *Oh well, I guess if I can get across, I can at least see my friends.* He focused on the shadow on the opposing dock and pictured himself there with all his heart and his power. Maybe it was his desire to see Hannah because the moment her face paused through his mind, he felt a rush far more violent than any that he felt in Zanier's study. The power was not his own—it lasted only a second as it had with all the other times. It was almost as if all the power in the darkness was his. He passed through the abyss before he felt firmness of the deck under his feet.

"*Alex!*" Will hugged him so firmly that he removed all the air from his lungs.

"Hey, Will."

"Everyone's down below—come on."

CHAPTER 6

Charles had more or less gotten used to Zanier's rages. As the one who primarily took part in the operations, he felt necessary—but that might not fit his image as the pious and powerful leader of the new age of magic.

"You got her?" Charles shrank back a bit—this was a bad rage he was entering.

"Yes, she came rather willingly. What happened? I wasn't expecting you till at least noon," he said, deciding to take it upon himself to soothe Zanier's mood with some good news.

"Damn him! I don't understand his power at all. It's even more different than I could ever have imagined. He's not even that gifted—his power can be no greater than an average mage!"

"Then why the concern?"

"When I taught him to fly, he didn't just use his power. He used it to control the air—no mage has ever done that—and all he did was give his crooked little smile when he fell back to the ground. It hardly took him any more effort than it takes us to fly."

"Oh …" This was genuine amazement at Alex's gifts. Though mages could enchant things to move—as long as they kept feeding it magic—they could never directly control elements with their power.

"He isn't even that good at it yet. I let him teleport to the other boat alone. He was able to do it fine in here."

"You what?" All concern left Charles' voice. *What's Zanier thinking? Is he going mad?*

"I have a feeling it'll be no trouble at all for him. He had no trouble at all with learning it. No mishaps at all—perfect every time," Zanier said. Charles was pleased to see Zanier calming himself. "I'll have Tantalus wait for him to come back over. He's rather eager to meet his prize—plus he wants a one up on Kyle."

The name Tantalus sent a shiver up Charles' spine. If there was one person in Zanier's little organization that he feared, it was Tantalus. He was also Kyle's one true rival in terms of power among the war mages. Where Kyle was calm and even mannered, Tantalus was a firestorm. He had challenged Kyle to a duel once for competition over who was the head of the war mages—he believed that since he was senior, it should be his. It was only through Zanier's power that the duel didn't destroy the dome. Despite a calm manner, Kyle knew when to be aggressive. Tantalus was just plain destructive in general, but he did have unprecedented sense and, despite his manner, his spells were incredibly under control. He and Kyle were at it for an hour before it was obvious that Kyle would win. Tantalus wouldn't give in and tried to bring the dome down on Kyle. It failed horribly, but the mere thought that he had tried to kill another was worth noting. Charles was careful to watch his words—and back—around that man. He also hated the idea of him being able to feel a mage of average strength from a mile away. It was impossible to sneak up on him.

"You sure it wasn't his idea?" Charles said to Zanier.

"I can't say he never hinted at it—plus it'll keep him in place for a while longer. Don't worry. All he's doing is bringing Alex a bulletproof suit and cape and one of our long knives just in case—and it's not a mission worth giving him a firearm. Now is when it all begins."

Charles swallowed as Zanier entered the room where he had brought Hannah. He had no idea what Zanier thought— he just tried to stay on his good side. *Oh, well. I hope he doesn't get too carried away.*

✳   ✳   ✳

Alex was embraced rather ferociously when he entered his friend's cabin. On his way down, he had earned some stares from other passengers—especially from those few who had been on deck when he'd been taken.

"Where's Hannah?" Alex asked anxiously.

"You didn't see her?" Karla asked, having just finished hugging him and returning to Mike's side.

"She went across with a taller guy in green robes—" Naomi was cut off by her brother.

"They all have green robes, stupid."

"Shut up, Sam. Oh, he had graying hair too. He seemed all weird."

"Charles … did he say why?"

"She's a mage," Mike answered.

Alex was shocked. "Really?"

Apparently, this was news for Will as well. "When did this happen?"

Karla said, "Alex, when you go back, make sure to go see her."

"I can't. I have to leave immediately. When I head back, Zanier wants me to do something for him."

James said, "Show us some magic!"

Alex had planned what to do for an answer. He surrounded himself with darkness. Alex smiled at this showy waste of power, but everyone gasped.

"Back up, please." Alex strolled over to the dresser and picked up a pencil and, with the mirror, he focused on its shadow and applied his will and bent it. Alex was satisfied when another series of gasps came.

"Cool!" Sam was jumping up and down.

Everyone except Mike was absolutely amazed.

"So you learned to control it?"

Alex opened his mouth to say something—letting the aura of darkness fade—but he couldn't think of anything.

Karla slapped Mike. "Ow"

"Leave him alone—his powers aren't evil."

"You weren't there!"

Everyone became silent.

"Mike, it hasn't happened since whatever it was. It doesn't affect me anymore."

"What—what happened?" James asked, confused at the sudden change of mood.

"I lost control of my powers. When I tried to call them on my own, I lost control, blasted two mages, and tried to drain the life out of Zanier. But I control it now, so it's safe."

"Alex, we knew. We didn't want to tell the younger ones," Karla said.

Sam and Naomi must have thought it was cool to blast people with magic and were now wrestling with James. Karla was staring angrily at Mike who still rubbed his face.

"At least you can control it—I wish I could do that," Simon said to liven up Alex again.

"Well, I have to go."

Simon and Will followed him while Mike was dragged by Karla into the other room. He could hear her erupt on Mike after they shut the door.

"It's okay, man. We'll make sure no one gets into any trouble while you're gone," Simon said, patting his shoulder.

"Except Mike with Karla," Will said. They all laughed and talked the rest of the way to the deck. He bid them farewell and, turning to the opposite deck, teleported.

"Hello there."

Alex looked at the one who had caught him with the stun blast on the boat. "I am to bring you to shore—rather far ashore at that. I have the gear you will need and I will brief you to your objective." He smiled as if amused at how official he sounded. "You will be performing the act of thievery on the Republic's largest gold supply. You will make your assault on some of the most impressive technological defenses of this time. You will have no support—if you fail, you will die. You will be given a bulletproof suit and a long knife—a far more appropriate weapon than a gun if you ask me—for your defenses if your powers fail you. You will be robbing … Fort Knox!"

❋   ❋   ❋

"Hello, Hannah."

"Hello, is Al—"

"He's gone on a very special operation for me and won't be back for a while."

"Oh," Hannah's mood suddenly shifted. This change was obvious.

"Oh, don't be so sad—this will give us time to train. You want your little boyfriend to be surprised to find out that not only are you a mage, but a mage possibly more powerful than he is."

Hannah's face went red—exactly as Zanier had planned.

CHAPTER 7

Alex gazed over the hillside at the fortress ahead of him. Adjusting his cloak in the wind, he comprehended what he was about to do. *I'm robbing Fort Knox.* He mentally checked over his power, making sure everything was still under control—and then his bulletproof cloak, and jumpsuit. *Let's hope I won't need any of this.* Everything was snug.

Tantalus had given him a brief tour of the ship's barracks, giving him what he believed necessary for the mission. Moving his hand over the hilt of his long knife, Alex liked it. He had no idea how to use a gun, but he was familiar with knives and blades. He crept closer, making sure his shadows were constantly shielding him from sight—and motion-sensing devices. He and Zanier had rigorously perfected this useful technique. He laughed to himself at how blatantly obvious it was that Zanier had planned this since he had seen Alex turn himself invisible.

God, it's cold! Olin fixed his jacket so it fit better. *God, I'm getting to old for this stuff.* Olin thought back to all he'd done in his life *Wow! I am old.* He'd started fighting in this war about nine years ago—except on the other side. *I was stupid back then.*

Damn those backstabbers! He had fought on the side of the New Americans till the New Americans had dragged his wife off a bus, leaving their son on board. *How old was he then? How old is he now?* He felt a tear well up. *Sixteen or seventeen—if he's still alive.* They had executed his wife on the spot, suspecting her as a traitor and then almost assassinated him before they realized their mistake. *Too late!* He had actually become a traitor and was now trying to avenge his wife. *They had to take me off the front lines and make me one of their army of guardsmen here.* Fort Knox had become a greatly important fortress to the Republic. Within the last year, they'd tripled the number of guards there, growing ever more paranoid about its safety.

Olin walked around the grounds with the other twenty-four guards on patrol tonight. *Who in their right mind would be able to break in here?* He assessed Fort Knox's defenses—that he knew of—and found no way a normal human could get into this place without an army behind him. The New Americans hadn't been successful militarily in a while, lacking the funds to launch another of the offensive surges that had gotten them so far. *Why does this cold remind me of something?*

✳ ✳ ✳

Alex moved slowly—and close to the ground—as silently as possible. Making sure that the lights were too far away to bother him, he knew that even if all the spotlights were fixed on him, they wouldn't see him. The dark silhouette would raise enough suspicion. If they investigated, they would most likely see him through the silhouette of shadow. He didn't want to have to fight—at least not *yet*. He needed to retain enough energy to teleport all the gold in the fort to the place Tantalus had landed with him on the New American coast.

The terrain was littered with boxes of ammunition, tanks, and other craft of war. Moving silently between them, he heard the sound of an approaching guard and stopped. The man appeared incredibly uncomfortable. Alex leaned up next to a crate and focused on cloaking himself with shadow. *Did I make noise? No, I was perfectly silent. Why is he stopping?*

※　※　※

The cold had just intensified. *Why is it so cold? It's only early October?* Olin stooped and wrapped his hands around himself. He adjusted his assault rifle and was surprised to find it comfortable—not incredibly cold—as he would suspect it to be with the temperature. Slowly he started walking again.

※　※　※

Good—he's going. Alex stepped away from the crate and continued on. Now standing directly behind the man—not five feet away—the guard stopped again. He was nervous that his stealth wasn't as good as he expected.

※　※　※

Confused, Olin stopped again. The temperature had just warmed and then cooled drastically. The temperature was staying steady again. *Cold! I must be going crazy.* Olin started walking again.

※　※　※

Alex took a deep breath and took off running. He just wanted to get away from that guard and barely dodged the outside of a spotlight in his haste.

* * *

The temperature changed again. This time, Olin looked over his shoulder. There was nothing. *Wait ... never mind.* Olin thought he had seen the outside of the beam flicker, but he dismissed it. *Humph? It's getting warmer. That's strange. Oh well, I won't complain.*

* * *

Alex moved quickly to the front and looked for the best way in. He saw that one of the windows was fairly shaded. *That'll work.* Focusing on his power, he lifted himself off the ground and carefully carried himself to the window. Looking inside, he saw a desk with an attractive young girl standing behind it. *She can't be much older than I am.* After a second or two, Alex regained his focus and saw two doors. The room was well furnished and comfortable. *Some fortress.* Turning his focus to the window, he started manipulating its matter so it would move out of his way.

* * *

Molly had been working all night and was exhausted. She had been filing a stack of papers and headed out the door. She straightened her dress as she passed through the door and frowned because it felt tighter than the previous time she had worn it. She hadn't been out much since her father started her here when the last secretary left, complaining about the long hours and pore wages. She had been really athletic throughout high school and wasn't used to not exercising all the time. She hadn't worn the dress since high school. It wasn't overly tight—just enough for her to notice.

She left through the door on her left, as Alex slipped through the window. He jumped off the windowsill and quickly dashed through the door the girl had just walked through. As he passed, he looked her over carefully. Her auburn hair was beautiful. She wore a simple blue dress that clung tightly around her slender curves. In perfect silence, he swept by her and into the corner of the room where the slight shadow would supply him sufficient camouflage.

Molly thought that she felt a breeze and quickly scanned the room, but she saw nothing except one of the corners was darker than usual. She placed the papers down on the table and headed back to the front. As she walked through the door, she smiled at an approaching man.

"Hey, Olin. How's your night going?" she said sweetly.

"As best it can, Molly. Beautiful as always." Molly smiled at the old man's compliment. "Is it just me or is it cold in here?"

"What do mean? It's not cold."

"Oh, I think I'm just getting too old for this."

Alex examined the solid steel door before him. He had gotten through the door from the second room easily enough, but this one was way too big to warp a hole through unnoticed. He could try teleporting, but he didn't want to blindly. He had no idea how thick it was—or who he might bump into—plus there were a ton of guards he could hear on the other side and about a million cameras trained on the door.

He could hear some people moving in through the corridor behind him. *Oh well, time to screw stealth—let's have some fun.* Removing his shadow cloak, he heard all sorts of alarms blaring. Smiling crookedly, he ignored a guard yelling and blew the door right off its hinges and back twenty feet into a group of approaching guards.

Behind him, he heard a guard start swearing before opening fire. The bullets were deflected by the shield of faint shadow that Alex had raised. Taking off, he ran down the maze of hallways, throwing guards left and right as they came at him. Finally, he reached an impressive door with all sorts of coded locks and scanners. The sound of bullets ricocheting off his shield was music to his ears. He focused his energy into lifting the door, tearing out everything else with it, and throwing it behind him. He sidestepped it as it swept into the crowd of assailants.

Alex stood in awe. *All this—and it was so easy.* Focusing on every ounce of the radiant gold, he forced his will upon it and told it where he wanted it to be. All the gold disappeared. Suddenly fatigued, Alex turned around and saw that another group of guards had formed—most were confused and awestricken. Alex sized them up. *Eight—not bad, but I'm exhausted.*

"What the hell is he?"

"I don't know but let's bury lead in his ass! Fire!"

Alex hadn't realized how tired he was until the bullets broke his shield and he felt the first rounds slam into his cape. He lifted his cloak so it would cover his head and knelt down. Immense pain filled his body as bullets hit his bulletproof suit. After what seemed like a lifetime, he heard their guns empty.

As he stood up, he could feel pain in every corner of his body, but he managed to smile at the guards. Drawing his long knife, he said, "I am a shadow mage—now you die!"

Charging them, he quickly cut down the first two. They tried to reload, but it was futile—Alex was too fast. Three, four, five—three more. Alex felt a sting on his chest as he cut down six and seven. Turning, he saw that the eighth had a sidearm that was now almost level with Alex's head. Alex struck at the man's wrist, removing nerves, blood vessels, and a chunk of bone. He drove his blade through the man's eyes into his head.

Alex examined his kill as he ran down the hall the way that he had come in. Near the end, he saw the first guard at the end of the hallway.

* * *

Olin stood shocked as he gazed into the eyes of a boy—a boy near the age of the one he had, same age as Molly. *How had he gotten all this way and where were all the guards?* He recognized the face—he recognized the face that he had not seen in a long time and a strange joy filled him. *My son. Why is he still charging? What is that cold? It's him. Oh my God! I felt him outside. I felt him when I came in. That knife—he's going to ... Oh my god. He doesn't know me.*

"Ugh ... my son," Olin grasped his stomach and felt cold steel.

* * *

Why isn't he firing? Alex charged down the hallway at the guard. *What is that look on his face?* Alex raised his knife ready to run through the man. *Is he happy?* He stabbed the man. *Did he say?*

"My son."

Stunned, Alex stepped back against the wall and watched the man die. *My father. Could he really be?* He recognized the dying man from so long ago, and he remembered his father's name.

"Olin Savadora … My father, I … I killed him." The girl standing before him was staring at him.

"He was your … You killed …" Her voice was scared and the hallway echoed with the sound of helicopters in the background. Alex grabbed her arm, focused all his remaining energy, and teleported them.

CHAPTER 8

Alex rolled over, hitting something hard with his head. He was instantly awake. He rolled around for a second, clutching his head. *Why does this hurt so much? I just hit a rock.* Suddenly he remembered the night before and wasn't sure that he wanted the pain to stop. *My father? How could I kill him? The girl!* She was gone! *Big surprise—she's probably horrified.* He groaned angrily at her for forcing him to use his power when he had obviously exhausted himself the night before. He was quite sure that this wasn't where he was supposed to meet Zanier. Thick pines surrounded him. This definitely was not the forest of Florida's panhandle, which was where they were supposed to meet. Alex laughed at how stupid he was. *How had I expected to get myself all the way down there? Fort Knox is probably just a few hundred yards north of here.* Alex let out a pulse of power and was surprised to sense the girl about four miles away to the southwest.

Alex started running. It was too far to teleport or fly with how weak he was. Instead, Alex used his power to replace his physical energy. Taking off in a full sprint, he could easily keep this pace up for thirty miles with the power he had left.

Alex sent out another pulse to the place where he had sensed her last and was impressed again to find her not only traveling in a straight line, but another three quarters of a mile farther southwest. *Pretty good for being in a dress and most likely barefoot by now.*

Alex found her curled up against the foot of a tree crying. His heart broke as he looked her over. Her dress was ripped almost all the way from leg to waist—as well as in numerous other places. Her hair was a mess. She still looked beautiful, but in a different way than at Fort Knox. She looked up at him in absolute horror and defiance.

"You monster! Why didn't you just kill me like the rest of them? Like your father!" Alex's strength left him as he leaned next to a tree and let the girl go off on him. He knew how much he deserved it. "He was a good man. Most of them were—they were doing their job."

"As was I."

She instantly hated him for the remark.

"Job! Attacking and killing people for gold! Where is it anyway? I didn't see you come out with it! Did you teleport it like you did us?—or do you like sneaking into top-security places and killing? Are you some New American special operative son of a bitch?"

"How do you think I feel? I just fucking killed my father. I had no idea—I hadn't seen him in nine years or more— that's when my mom was pulled off a bus and probably shot. I've spent that entire time on my own while you lived your wealthy fucking life! Don't even fucking try to deny that! How much did that dress cost?"

"How many children did you just render fatherless? How many did you give the same fate as yourself? How can you not care? You're a monster! How can someone like you have a father like Olin? You deserve the fate of killing your own father! I only hate that Olin recognized you before he died!"

Alex struck her across the face. She surprised him by jumping on him. A minute earlier, she had been horrified of him and now she was fighting him as if she was his physical equal. He was even more surprised by the force in which he hit the tree behind him. He grabbed her waist and threw her behind him past the tree. He walked slowly over to her on the ground and realized that her cheek was bleeding where he had hit her. Feeling kind of badly, he went to help her and was surprised when she kicked out his legs, knocking him to the ground. She was instantly on top of him and, before he could react, she punched him on the left side of his face. He rolled her over so that he was on top. Alex realized that this wasn't the first time she had done this. She continued to roll, using his momentum to get herself back on top. It should have worked, but there was a ledge and a ten-foot drop into a small clearing. After the fall, they tried to catch their breath.

The sound of clapping from the opposite side of the clearing caught Alex's attention. Alex quickly got to his feet and the girl was only a little slower. "My, my—now I've seen everything. The great shadow caster rolling around on the ground with some girl—not to mention an ungifted and untrained one."

"Who are you?" Alex asked. The man was middle aged; his hair was faded auburn and gray at the temples. His face was strongly handsome and barely showed his age. His eyes were dark with hints of reds, oranges, and greens. He was lean and just over six feet tall.

"Hmm … a long time since I was asked that. I've been called many things: devil's magus, demon of light, something Italian meaning son of a bitch. You can call me Lasorian. It's the name that most who still know of my existence would call me, but you should really know that I'm one of the only warlocks left."

"Zanier never said—"

"Zanier has never said a lot of things—for reasons his own—but he knows full well of my existence."

"What do you want? What's a warlock?"

"A warlock is someone who has bonded his soul with that of a demon's to gain magical ability." That didn't sound too good to Alex. "As for what I want, I'm more honest than most so I'll put it simply—to deprive Zanier of you and keep the one hope of this world alive."

"What do you mean one hope of this world? I'm just a shadow mage!"

"Just! And it is shadow caster—you are nothing close to a mage. You are much greater. Do you have any idea how much power you wield!"

"I almost died trying to rob Fort—"

"It's because Zanier is a fool and is too blind to realize how much power you can control. He is too afraid to imagine such power—all that is darkness is yours and all the shadows of the universe are at your disposal. Do you have any idea how many shadow casters have ever existed? Twelve! You are one the most powerful beings to ever walk this earth. Armies have fallen at the feet of shadow casters. Whenever one has been born—with one exception—their power rocked the foundations of the world. You have yet to realize what you truly are."

"How did a pitiful creation like you get so lucky? Ha! I have no idea what you're all talking about, but I want to go home," Molly said.

"You can't," Alex responded quietly.

"Well, she could, but the RUSA would be all over her with questions about Alex here. Smartest thing he ever did was to bring you with him—basically saved your life."

"One life he did save."

"What's RUSA?"

"Republic of the United States of America. Where did you grow up?" Molly asked.

"In the slums of New England. The New America is a lot less formal with the titles of their enemies," Lasorian answered.

"Oh," Molly said.

"Tell me what's going on. Why would Zanier lie to me? Why am I here? How do you know so much about me?"

"Well, to understand everything, you need to understand why Zanier is doing what he is doing—and that has to do with the history of magic."

The girl sighed as she leaned up against the embankment.

"The origin of magic is unknown; the most primitive forms were that of shamans that cast spells to help fertilize the land and cure wounds and illnesses. They were no more than mages with a more basic knowledge of their powers. It wasn't until the infancy of the Greek and Persian Empires that the mages' powers were divided into the three types that you know about. It was also at the beginning of this time that the first shadow caster appeared. You might have heard of him. He was the great Persian king, Cyrus I—you may know the name. It was also in this time that the first sorcerer appeared. A sorcerer is a spell caster that is able to cast spells, use invocations, and use spells that do not require a magic reserve. The second shadow caster came around not to long after the fall of the Persian empire to Alexander the Great. He merely lived as a slave in China—until his family was threatened. He destroyed half the town—including himself—but managed to save his child and wife. The next step for magic was the birth of the warlock—the evolution of the sorcerer who found a way to bind their souls to demons. This gave them magical abilities beyond their own advanced yet time-consuming spells. They could get the same results instantaneously. They could also perform binding multiple times, making themselves the superior to the mages and changing the face of magic. This ignited a hate that still exists today. The birth of the Roman Empire also gave rise to two of the greatest shadow casters of all time: the Romulus and Remus. The brothers had a final duel for power that was even more theatrical than the common legend. They rocked the foundations of the universe as all the darkness in the universe was split between them. It wasn't till Romulus tricked his brother with a draw that he buried a knife into his back.

"The Roman Empire would give us three more shadow casters—all whose names were forgotten to most, but were the sole reason for their success. The birth of Christ and the spread of Christianity would eventually reshape the world—but with unpredictable results. The condemnation of magic began after the barbarians sacked Rome and the Middle Ages. A prominent shadow caster—the eighth in history—made a name for himself with his powers. He traveled to Rome and demanded that the pope use his influence to send aid to the Middle East where persecution in Jerusalem of spell casters had already begun. It was here that the pope damned the shadow caster to death and the hardship for all spell casters began. The shadow caster on the spot bound himself to the darkness and cursed the pope that he would haunt him for all his life. Whenever darkness neared, he disintegrated himself in a burst of dark power. In return for their protection, mages and warlocks alike provided aid to the Muslims against the Crusaders. You see, the Pope had convinced all the people in the West that anyone who practiced magic traffics with demons. This is only true for warlocks, but a good warlock isn't corrupted by the spirit he binds—he merely claims its powers. The witch hunts began and decimated the population of magic users. They reduced the frequency of births of shadow casters. Nearly four hundred years after the last shadow caster was born, the Spanish Inquisition began. Though founded under false pretenses, the reason for its existence was that they found out the secret bloodline of shadow casters—and set out to hunt down and kill all who had shared it. They did not hesitate to kill any spell casters they discovered. Their main goal, though secret, never changed. They eventually discovered who they believed to be the last descendent of shadow caster blood and sentenced him to death. He was a twenty-two-year-old man with a wife. He had an unknown child with a mistress, but that child would be forever ignored by history—as would the event that led to the death of the ninth shadow caster. When his execution began, his powers awoke and he leveled the facility. He killed many important people behind the Inquisition. It never recovered and the bloodline continued, making its way to North America. It flared up in a certain writer who wrote poetry about the visions that his half-developed powers brought him. It destroyed his sanity and led to his death—I believe his name was Edgar Allen Poe.

"Now magic is no more—it no longer exists in the minds of most people. It's become some kind of fantasy from long ago for stories, movies, and video games. Our minds were so driven away from it that even the eleventh shadow caster—your grandfather, Alex—never so much as felt a wink of his power. It was then that I allowed myself to wonder whether all was lost, but then a miracle happened—you. For the first time in history, a shadow caster was born within two generations of the last."

Alex couldn't believe what he had heard—all his history lessons had been completely revised in less than twenty minutes.

"Liar," Molly said. "There is no way that could be true. You're all crazy!"

"It makes sense," Alex responded.

"How?"

Alex was surprised at her drastic change from being absolutely terrified to arguing with them.

"You look like a smart girl. Tell me why this isn't true. Why should you take the word of well-educated and manipulated people over me? He's just some guy that you met in the woods. Honestly there's no difference anymore."

She let out a sigh and went back to leaning on the embankment.

"Alex—"

"You never answered my question. How do you know so much about me?"

"Because you are important. I have many means of gathering information."

"We're leaving."

"*We're?* You mean you and the girl. Where are you going? Back to Zanier?"

"My friends are there."

"Hannah too. I guess ... well, I can't allow that."

"What are you going to do, stop me? By the way, how'd you know I'd be here?"

"Simple. I pulled you out of your teleport. The only reason I couldn't get you to land right here was that you gave unnecessary resistance to my magic. I influenced the girl's mind a little and got her to run here. It was by chance that you fell down the ditch."

"You did *what* to my mind?"

Alex began focusing on teleporting. Realizing that he didn't have enough power, he remembered what Lasorian had said and focused on the shadows of the trees around him. He tried pulling their power to him—it was a shockingly large amount of power. It refreshed and strengthened him. Lasorian noticed.

"Oh, that's it. Notice how the shadows flicker and shrink at your call?"

Alex walked over to the girl and placed his hand on her shoulder. She didn't pull back; she knew what Alex was doing and wanted to be gone as much as he did. He hesitated. The touch of her warm flesh nauseated him for a second—not like when Hannah had embraced him. It was something different that he had not felt the night before.

"I can't allow you to leave."

"Stop me!" Alex started to teleport, focusing on the spot that Tantalus had shown him—and then ... pain.

Molly screamed and tripped over a rock. Alex was pinned against the embankment by an unseen force, writhing in pain. Lasorian was making weird hand signals and chanting under his breath.

Molly yelped again as she realized that all the shadows of the tress were bending toward Alex and he was giving off a faint dark aura.

"That's it, shadow caster. Call the darkness to you. Wield it against me! Break my enchantment! End your pain!" He was laughing now—not a crazy laugh—but one of being legitimately entertained. It still scared Molly more than anything else that was going on.

"Stop it! Stop hurting him!"

"Didn't you hate him? Don't you want him to suffer for what he did?"

"I did. I don't want him to anymore. He killed his father. I saw it in his eyes. I wanted him to be a monster so I could have someone to blame, but I don't … I don't want … I don't hate him … anymore."

"You changed your mind fast." He laughed and released the spell. Alex fell to the ground unconscious. "Take this." Lasorian threw her a key to room 212 in an apartment on Ceruse Street about a hundred yards away." He pointed toward the opposite side of the clearing. "You'll have to carry him. Try to make sure no one sees you two—that'll make quite the sight."

"Um … okay. Won't the owners—"

"They're never there. They pay people to do everything for them. All they care about is getting their money, and I'll take care of that."

Lasorian helped Molly lift Alex up, but left immediately and disappeared into the woods. Molly carried Alex the rest of the way.

Chapter 9

Alex woke on a bed feeling quite comfortable. Slowly he remembered what had happened. He found himself in a small room that he didn't recognize. It was empty except for a girl in the corner. She was wearing a bathrobe and combing her wet hair with a large smile.

"Get up! Hurry! By the way, my name is Molly."

She walked over to the bed and sat down. "Hurry!" Alex couldn't help but to notice that she had very nice legs.

"Where are we?"

"I don't know—some town, some road named Ceruse Street. I don't care—they have a mall and we're going out."

"What? Why?"

"Because you can't go running around everywhere in a jumpsuit or the same clothes every day. You smell bad enough already. Hurry. Go take a shower. Your clothes are already in the bathroom."

Alex started halfheartedly rolling off the bed only to find himself violently shoved against the wall.

"What was that for?"

Molly had taken his spot on the bed. Her answer was sticking her tongue out at him. Since he was up, he slowly trudged the rest of the way to the bathroom.

Molly laughed as Alex closed the bathroom door. She put on the short skirt and tank top that she had found. She was surprised that everything fit.

Alex walked out wearing a pair of jeans and black T-shirt of some band he had never heard of. He stopped for a second when he saw Molly.

"How do I look?"

"Great."

She smiled. "Guys always say that."

"Well, it's true."

Alex wasn't lying; he could hardly stop looking at her. Hannah was more slender and delicate. Her beauty almost clashed with Molly's slender, curvy body that radiated confidence.

"You could try something like gorgeous or pretty or cute or even stunning—not always good or great."

She opened the top drawer of the cabinet and threw two stacks of bills at him. They were hundreds.

"Where did these come from?" Alex had never seen so much cash in his life.

"The drawer is full of them—and money from other countries too. Here's some from China, here's some from Russia, and there's a bunch of Euros."

Alex walked over to the cabinet. She was right—there had to be millions of dollars in all types of currency.

"How?"

"I don't know—Lasorian just handed me the key to this place. Guess he didn't leave us empty-handed." She grabbed his arm, but Alex hesitated for a second. "Come on—it'll be fun. Don't worry—I won't tell that Hannah girl." She smiled and pulled Alex toward the door.

✳   ✳   ✳

Will paced the dock, thoroughly convinced that he would never step on a boat again. He'd been uneasy since Alex left and Hannah had come over once—just four days later—and the changes had happened swiftly. Mages traveled over to their boat more and more often and took over as the authority—much to the captain's complaints. The captain had demanded from the start that the mages let the boat go—once they had made it clear that they meant no harm. Karla and Mike were constantly with each other and—like everyone else on the ship—constantly on the deck, desperate to get out of the cramped and increasingly smelly cabins. The crew had completely given up on taking care of the boat and its passengers—except for emergencies. The mages were now even supplying food.

"Hey, Will," said Simon.

"Hey."

"James is taking care of Naomi and Sam." Will had to laugh. "Don't worry, I locked the door."

"The door locks from the outside?"

"The closet does," Simon said. Will almost broke out laughing. "They were playing in there so I didn't think they'd mind it too much. It's ventilated—they'll be fine."

"Yeah," Will said.

"We need to get out of here," Simon said seriously.

"Yeah, how?" Will said sarcastically. "We don't even know where the hell we are."

"Hannah might."

"Hannah? Hannah has shown her head once in four days. Yes, I know Alex was gone for over a week, but Alex was still Alex when he came back. Hannah was totally different. She was all mages this and mages that. 'Oh, I can't wait for Alex to see what I can do.'"

"I've known Hannah longer than you have."

"Kinda—and we both know she isn't like this ever."

"She has hope!"

Will was shocked at Simon raising his voice. "For once she has hope, Will. She has never had that before—even in Alex. All she has needed is something to place hope in. Alex did for the longest time, but now she has the mages—and they give her more than Alex could."

"She's wrong. I don't like these mages," Will said.

"She'll help us—she can get us a dinghy or something and allow us to get to shore."

"No, she won't. It's Alex we need—not her."

"Alex is god-knows-where doing whatever that Zanier guy told him to do."

"I'm not sure."

"About what?" Simon asked.

"Something's wrong," Will said softly. "Something went wrong."

"What do you mean?"

"Just after Alex left, something changed in the mages. Why isn't he back yet?"

"He's probably not done yet."

"I don't know—it just doesn't seem right. Alex didn't make it seem like it was gonna take long."

"You think he's ... dead."

"No. Well ... maybe. I don't know, but I doubt he's coming back to the mages."

❋　❋　❋

Zanier was furiously pacing in his study to calm himself. *That insolent Lasorian—what could he want? Why now? He's going to mess up everything.* Hannah, Kyle, Sara, and Charles entered his study.

He'd been involving Hannah in these meetings as much as possible. She had shocked everyone when her powers were that of a war mage and her talent reviled any mages on the boat. She had been training constantly with Kyle and Zanier since joining them.

"You wanted us," said Sara. Her humor had recently gone downhill. Zanier suspected that it was all the time he demanded of Kyle.

Zanier fingered the letter that Tantalus had given him for Lasorian. The red sunset wasn't wholly visible. "Alex isn't coming back."

Charles said, "What do you mean? He succeeded. He got the gold. Did he get in trouble escaping?"

"No. He escaped. It seems he's turned traitor on us. Lasorian sent me this."

Sara's pale face went another shade whiter. She was the only one in the room who knew of Lasorian.

Hannah said, "What do you mean? Alex wouldn't leave—all his friends are here. And me and training. What happened?"

"I thought he was—" Sara said.

"Dead? I thought he was too. You were a child when it happened, but he survived—and it seems he isn't done yet."

"Who is Lasorian?" Kyle asked.

"A warlock," Zanier answered.

"You said they'd been destroyed!" Charles said.

"I thought they were gone. I fought him sixteen years ago. I thought I defeated him, but it turns out I was wrong. He was Sara's grandfather. She was six and I had started training her. He came one day to stop me. We fought. It seems he managed to escape. I thought he was dead."

Sara said, "I never saw him. My mom almost never talked about him. He suddenly showed up at some family thing for the first time. He seemed hell-bent on stopping Zanier. I begged him to stop. He lowered his shields against Zanier's attacks, but before Zanier could stop, they hit him. There were no remains. I thought—we all thought—he was dead."

"And what does he want with Alex?" Hannah asked.

"It isn't clear, but he somehow managed to convince him not to return."

"What are we going to do?" Kyle asked.

"You and Charles need to go find him and bring him back." Zanier dropped the letter then said to Sara, "What do you want?"

"You better know what you're doing," Zanier said.

Sara left quickly and Kyle rushed after her.

"You two can leave." Hannah started to say something, but was nudged by Charles as they left.

Zanier sighed once they were gone. *Lasorian, what do you want now? What is it about Alex that I don't know?*

＊   ＊   ＊

Alex couldn't believe that it was humanly possible to get so excited about clothes. Molly drifted from one side of the store to the other faster than Alex could keep track. She kept picking up more and more. Alex swore that she must have had half the store in her arms when she finally decided to start trying stuff on. Alex slouched into a chair, thoroughly exhausted—and he had just watched.

The first thing she came out with was a red V-neck bra top and a pair of dark jeans.

"How do I look?" she asked, trying to walk around like a model.

"Umm ... good?" Alex said.

Molly smiled. "I got more."

Next she came out in a tight-fitting green and white polo and a different pair of jeans that Alex didn't notice. He was too preoccupied with how she'd gotten the polo on.

"Hmm ..." Molly looked into the mirror before turning to Alex. She puffed out her cheeks.

Alex laughed. "What?"

"I'm too fat," she said, patting her belly.

Alex hadn't noticed, but the polo did seem a little too tight around the waist. There was no way that could compare with how clearly stressed it was around her breasts, but the polo looked really small.

"Why not try a bigger size?"

"I used to always wear this size."

"In all honesty, you'd have to be a stick to wear that."

"Well, then I used to be a stick," Molly pouted, "Now I've got this and this and this," she said, patting her stomach and butt.

Alex had no idea what was wrong with her butt and had no idea how she could even call her slender figure fat. "You look great."

"Thanks," she said. "I guess I'll try the bigger size."

The night went on with Molly trying on what seemed to be an infinite amount of clothes and purchased almost every one. She forced Alex to buy at least six outfits, using the reason that he couldn't run around in a jumpsuit and the same pair of jeans and tie all the time. After about five different stores, they had used about half the money they'd brought, which Alex had previously thought impossible.

At this point, Molly was wearing a light green sundress, an outrageous straw sombrero, a pair of high heels that laced slightly up the lower leg, and a pair of shades. Alex was wearing the same thing as he'd walked in with. They ate dinner at a Chinese restaurant.

Molly was smiling and staring at Alex swirling the straw around in his soda.

"What?" Alex asked.

"It's been a while since I was on a date," Molly said. Her smile widened at Alex's reaction.

"Date?"

"Yeah. We shopped together and now we're getting dinner. What else would you call it?"

"Uh—"

"I guess we could see a movie too. A sappy romance."

Alex blushed and Molly laughed. "I guess I should be proud to make you blush, 'great shadow caster.' Seriously, my dad hasn't let me do much of anything since he was elected as a senator of Kentucky."

"Your dad's a what?"

"Senator. Yeah, he got elected because of his military background. He enlisted all my brothers to make himself look good. They're the ones that taught me to wrestle. There are three of them: Jack, Eddy, and Martin. I'm youngest. Even when I was in school, guys were afraid to ask me out because my brothers might beat them up. He didn't enlist me because I was supposed to be his perfect little angel. When the old secretary quit, my dad gave me the job. Twelve to twelve, every day except for Sunday. It was boring paperwork over and over again about the fort's condition, which—until you—was great."

Alex smiled. "Why did you to want to go back so badly then?"

"Because you scared the hell out of me. But as it turns out, you're just a shy guy who got lucky and is now—according to that weird guy in the woods—the most powerful being in the world. How old are you anyways?"

"I'm seventeen. My birthday was two days ago."

Alex lost his train of thought as his attention turned to the news. Molly followed his gaze.

CHAPTER 10

Mike almost didn't notice Karla's eyes changing from him to the TV screen behind his head. All the eyes in the dining hall—even those of his friends—turned to the news.

"My God," said Simon.

Hannah was combing her hair when she heard a knock on her door. A mage barged in and turned on the news. Hannah's mouth dropped.

✳ ✳ ✳

Kyle felt Sara tense in his arms as the news story changed. "Sara ..."

"It's Alex!"

✳ ✳ ✳

Tantalus ran up behind Charles.

"What?"

"You need to watch this." Tantalus grabbed Charles' arm and dragged him into the dining area. Charles' eyes went wide.

✳ ✳ ✳

Zanier heard commotion and opened the door to his study. Mages were rushing all around into others rooms that had TVs. From the hallway, he stared into one crowded room. It was a sight that no one would ever believe and he smiled.

"Breaking news from Kentucky as reports of a one-man assault on Fort Knox results in the theft of all its gold. Senator George Winfield has shared the following images captured on security cameras the night of the attack. You won't believe what you see."

Everyone was transfixed by the video of the heist.

"I know this is hard to believe, but what we see is real. Senator Winfield believes that some New American technology is responsible for the horror."

The second man said, "We also have sad news that the girl in these images is Senator Winfield's daughter, Molly Winfield. He also believes that the New American forces will hold her for ransom." Several images flashed of Molly in school photos and looking happy in a track outfit. "The loss of the gold at Fort Knox will have dire effects on the economy already struggling in this war-torn nation. Now to economy expert—"

✳   ✳   ✳

Alex couldn't believe what he had just seen on the TV—and neither could anyone else in the mall. People were yelling and babies were crying—as were some other economically savvy people who knew what the loss of all that gold would mean.

Alex was suddenly glad for Molly's shades and hat, which now covered her entire face. He was thankful that no clear shots of him had been shown. He grabbed Molly's hand and helped her up.

"Let's get out of here."

* * *

Kyle didn't move while Sara turned off the TV.

"See—that's why I don't want you to go after him."

"Alex wouldn't harm us—he's not like that."

"You said he can't always control his powers. What if he resists you? What if you and Charles force him to lose control?"

"Don't worry about me and Charles. We are a good team—I doubt even Alex could stop us."

Kyle's words seemed to have little effect on Sara. She buried her head in Kyle's chest.

* * *

"Hmm ..." said Charles.

"That fool! Why take the girl?" Tantalus responded.

"Seems that me and Kyle have our work cut out for us."

Tantalus smiled. "Make sure to drop your shields on him when Alex takes a swing at him—for me."

"Sorry, no can do. Sara would have my head—I fear her a bit more than you," Charles said.

* * *

Zanier turned back into his study. *So, Alex, you did good. I'm starting to see Lasorian's reason for being so interested in you.*

* * *

Molly had trouble keeping up with Alex because her heels kept getting in the way. She almost fell twice, but Alex still held her wrist. A burst of cold air hit Molly's face as he nearly dragged her out the mall. Her heel caught a doorstop, but Alex quickly caught her.

Dazed momentarily by their closeness, she tried to shake it off. His breath on her face didn't help. Molly felt Alex lift her and drag her around a corner. She smiled to herself about how self-conscious she was with his hands around her waist. For the second time, she felt the rush of air and the compressed feeling on her lungs that meant he had teleported them.

She could finally breathe again. They were in the corner of their room—still in the same position they had been in before he teleported them. Again, she became aware of his breath and exactly how close his lips were to hers. Alex suddenly pulled away.

"God!" Alex ran both hands through his hair. "I'm so stupid."

Molly wasn't entirely sure what he was talking about.

"They're gonna find out who I am, they must have video of when I ... when I killed my father. They didn't have audio on those videos, but they must on the originals."

Molly was suddenly aware that Alex hadn't felt anything near what she had. She was happy for the shades. She didn't know whether to slap him, run to the bathroom, or yell at him.

"At least your face wasn't all over the news! Now all of RUSA knows what I look like and will be sure to turn me in if they see me! Maybe I should turn myself in!" Alex was shocked, but Molly continued. "Why should I stay with America's most wanted? Not daring to show my head outside.

I'm starving and there's no food in here—plus the only clothes I have now is this!" She decided that the bathroom was a good destination. Not caring to see Alex's expression, she slammed the door behind her.

Chapter 11

Hannah couldn't sleep because her mind kept replaying the newscast. She decided to wander the halls of the ship. Making her way to the deck, she leaned over the railing to feel the water splashing and the mist hitting her face. The moon was almost full and all the stars were visible.

"Beautiful, isn't it?" Charles said from behind her.

"Yeah."

"I'm surprised to see you out here."

"I couldn't sleep."

"Me neither——then again, I haven't slept well for a while now."

"Why not?" Hannah asked.

"All the searching and plotting. Zanier hasn't taken it easy on anyone for a long time. Till now, it's been me, Kyle, and Sara taking the brunt of it."

He stared longingly out to sea.

"What do mean?"

"The search for you demanded a lot of drain on our powers, then the training of Alex and now you. Plus, Zanier has had plenty of things for me and Kyle to do—Tantalus also. I guess you'll find out soon enough."

Hannah stared silently out to sea.

"I'm not feeling too good about mine and Kyle's next task."

"Alex?"

"After watching that news feed, I'm starting to worry about how Kyle and I will do against him—especially if he attacks as ruthlessly as he did at Fort Knox."

"Alex won't harm you."

"I hope you're right, but if he refuses to come, we're supposed to use force. I'm not sure how he'll respond to that."

"I know Alex."

"Maybe—but how well do you know what his powers will do? He's not entirely in control—you know that."

"His powers?"

"Have a mind of their own—they might even be controlling him now."

When he left, Hannah worried whether Alex was under control of his powers.

*   *   *

Charles smiled to himself as he walked away. *Oh, how I love deception.* He was worried about one thing—he didn't want to be forced to confront Alex. He knew that he and Kyle were more powerful then Alex, but he couldn't help but worry.

*   *   *

Molly could no longer think of anything else to do in the bathroom to keep herself from confronting Alex again. She limped to the door; she'd managed to twist her left ankle in the escape. Opening the door, she was determined to still be mad at Alex.

Furiously thinking of something to accuse Alex of next, she lost her train of thought. All the clothes they'd bought were lying on the bed in their bags. Alex sat at a table opposite an empty chair. To Molly's shock, the food they had ordered was on the table.

"How did you do that?"

The smile vanished and was replaced by a more gentlemanly expression. "Why don't you have a seat? You said you were hungry."

Molly sat down.

"How did you do this?" Molly said before taking a bite of her salad.

"It wasn't that hard—the clothes were right where we'd left them. And the waiter was bringing our food at the same time I got there." He began digging into his food.

"What about the chairs and the table?" Molly said.

"Nothing is that hard to get a hold of when you can turn invisible and bend matter," he said.

"You stole it!"

"They were in the storeroom to these apartments—I'll bring them back," Alex said.

"Didn't you say it was your birthday two days ago?"

"Yeah."

"Happy birthday!" Molly said.

"Thanks."

"Tomorrow I'm baking you a cake," Molly said.

Alex looked surprised.

"Come on—it's a cake. Don't you have cake on your birthday?" Molly felt badly as she remembered his history.

"The last real birthday party I had was when I was six."

"Oh …" Molly said. *Idiot!* "Well, you're going to have one tomorrow!" Alex smiled slightly at her persistence. "It'll be fun—don't worry."

After they ate, Alex moved the table and chairs into the corner of the room and spread blankets on the ground.

"We can share the bed—it's big enough."

Alex blushed. "I'll be fine."

Molly rolled her eyes. She pranced over to Alex and guided him to the right side of the bed. "You get this side. I get the other. If it bothers you so much, you can face away from me."

She smiled when Alex looked over his shoulder questioningly.

"There. Oh, turn around—I need to get changed. I'm not sleeping in this."

Molly dug through the bags until she found a knee-length nightgown. After changing, she turned around. Alex still faced the wall, but he'd taken off his shirt. Molly sucked in a quick breath, choking slightly as she saw Alex's back. All down the left side were large welts and bruises.

"What?"

"Your back!"

"Yeah, that's from when they were shooting me and I couldn't keep up a shield anymore."

"Are you going to do anything for them?"

"They're bruises. They're nothing serious. I can't really do anything for them anyways." Alex slid into bed and turned to face the wall. Molly watched his rhythmic breathing, unable to take her eyes off his back.

❋   ❋   ❋

Will and Simon decided that they had to talk to Karla and Mike about their plan to ask Hannah for help to get off the boat. Will was leaning on the wall when Simon entered with Karla and Mike.

Taking over the role of leader—as he'd done since Alex had been gone—Mike said, "Will, Simon says you two have been thinking of a way to get off the boat."

Though Mike's junior by several years, Will was never intimidated by him in his size or forceful manner. He thought it sounded weird when he took control. Alex was the only one in the group he'd ever truly follow. "Me and Simon both think that we can't stay here any longer—we don't trust the mages."

"And we all saw that news report," Simon said. "Alex got out of there and that had to be two days ago. It must have only taken him a day to get there."

"And we would know if he had gotten back by now," Will said.

Karla nodded before speaking. "You're right—I don't like the mages either."

"And how are we going to get off? Mages are everywhere on this boat—plus we don't have a clue where we are."

"Not true," Simon said. "If you paid attention to the location of the sun, you'd know that we're heading east—and have been for a while. Plus that news station must have been from the Republic. And we've seen land in the right places." Simon pulled a map from under one the beds. He made a circular motion with his finger around an area ten miles in radius about a hundred miles directly east of the point on Florida's panhandle. "We're somewhere in this area."

"Oh." Mike seemed awed that Simon had been able to do that. "Still, we're surrounded by water."

"That's were Hannah comes in," Simon said.

"Hannah?" said Karla.

"Simon wants her to help get one of those rescue boats down. She most likely won't be stopped—judging from how she said Zanier treats her."

"She won't help," Karla said. Simon and Mike were shocked.

"That's what I said," Will said.

Mike said, "But it's Hannah—she's our friend."

"But she loves the mages and the new powers the mages gave her. She'll forget all we've done for her."

"What about Alex? She loves him."

"And she still thinks she does, and actually might," Karla said somberly. "Wait till you see what will happen when she's forced to choose between him and the mages."

Simon was almost as lost as Mike had been. "She wouldn't dare choose the mages over Alex."

"I say we get one of the boats on our own. Hannah will probably end up informing Zanier and then we'll be locked up tighter than we already are."

"I can't believe you guys actually think she'd betray us," Simon said and left the room.

❄   ❄   ❄

Waking up, Alex tried to move his left arm, but it had stiffened up. He searched through the bags on the floor for clothes. Eventually, he came across a red tie and some jeans. Changing quickly, he looked over at Molly. She had managed to take up most of the bed and had her face squished on the pillow. Not a very attractive image, but endearing all the same. Alex had no intention for waiting for her to wake up and he quickly scribbled a note.

Molly,

Gone on a walk may be gone for a bit. Feel free to make the cake.

Alex

Alex quickly laced up his new running shoes and left. He wanted to speak with Lasorian. He needed to ask him some questions. He decided that the best place to start looking was the clearing. Having no memory of the trip to the apartment, he walked around the side of the complex into its shadow.

Reaching out with his powers, he could feel the energy surrounding him. He'd practiced using the power of other shadows last night in the escape from the mall and when he returned for the food and clothes. Though the building's shadow did not have nearly the amount of power as the complete darkness of night, he still felt strangely refreshed drawing on it—plus it offered ample power for what he needed.

Alex felt the rush of teleporting. He walked from under the shade of one of the many surrounding trees. As he approached the middle of the field, he heard a voice behind him.

"You've come back—that shouldn't be surprising. You have questions. What is it you wish to know?"

Alex saw Lasorian about ten feet behind him. "First, how safe is our location?"

"As safe as you make it. Those pictures of Molly on the news probably won't help. Keep her wearing hats and sunglasses—no one will suspect to see her around here."

"Where is here?"

"Tennessee—I believe the name of the town is Branchville."

"Does Zanier know where I am?"

"Not yet, but he will unless you act."

"What do you mean?"

"Tonight Zanier will land in Tampa ahead of his landing party. He's sending Kyle and Charles to quickly move up the continent, looking for leads on you. If they make it as far as Fort Knox, they're going to most likely head south again—but more carefully. Chances are if they make it as far as somewhere around here, they will pick up on huge amounts of magic."

"I can't be sensed."

"But I can—and I haven't taken many precautions on keeping down the auras given off by the many rituals and spells I've performed over the years—much to my fault."

Alex glared at Lasorian. "So they'll find this place anyway."

"Eventually, but not for a while—if you follow my instructions."

Alex waited.

"Cut them off before they can even leave Florida. Do something to attract their attention. Force them to engage you and overwhelm them. Make Zanier hesitate to send anyone one else after you."

Alex nodded. "I have one more question."

"Yes?"

"Why are you helping me?"

"Helping you? No. I have my own agenda. Helping you is merely convenient to me right now."

Alex smiled slyly. "Till next time." He started to walk away before turning back and saying, "By the way, which way is out of here?"

Lasorian smiled and pointed; Alex walked off in that direction.

✳   ✳   ✳

Molly immediately regretted opening her eyes as light blinded her. Rolling ungracefully out of bed, she realized that Alex wasn't there. It took a second before she found the note. *He could have woken me up.* Tossing the note back on the counter, she started unpacking the bags of clothes. *He could have put these away.* After putting away the clothes, she put on the bra top and jeans combo from the night before. There was no stove or oven—just a minifridge in the corner. *Well, that'll make it hard to bake a cake.* Grabbing the pen, she walked over to Alex's note and added.

No oven—hope you like store-bought!

She added a little smiley face. Running into the bathroom, she thanked her father's slowness. All the pictures he'd given the news were of her hair up looking like the perfect little schoolgirl. She was always dismayed at her hair's slight natural curl. However, she didn't think it looked half bad with the red top bringing out the red in her auburn hair. Grabbing her shades, she left the apartment.

✳   ✳   ✳

Alex expected to see Molly still in bed. Noticing that she was gone, he saw that she'd written something at the end of his note. Her handwriting was almost as bad as his was. He smiled as he read the note and decided to look for her.

❋ ❋ ❋

Zanier stared down at the map of Tampa spread out on the floor of his room. Kyle and Tantalus were arguing over how the assault would take place. Tantalus felt that—since he'd be in charge of the main assault in Kyle's absence—he should get the final word. Sara and Charles were also present. Charles was abnormally silent and Sara was brooding about Kyle leaving to hunt down Alex. Zanier knew what he wanted in the assault and both Kyle's and Tantalus's plans were giving it to him—a display of his power to the rest of the world.

"We can't throw all the war mages into the main assault. The guardian mages won't be able to keep up with them and we don't want any resistance fire getting through their shields. We have only a vague idea how much there will be," Kyle argued.

"So do you want to push with the guardians and have the war mages take the flanks?" Tantalus responded.

"Yes."

"That'll be too slow—they will have more time to organize resistance."

"Slow? We have all night—and what kind of resistance are they going to organize? Why risk taking casualties when we can sweep through them without any loss of life."

"Kyle's right—" Sara was cut off by Tantalus.

"Isn't that your job—to keep them from dying?" Tantalus said to Sara. "And what are they going to be able to hit us with if we clear through them before they fully understand what's happening?"

Hannah entered, taken aback by Tantalus' harshness. She had recently found a robe that fit her—she no longer stood out as the only one not in the green of Zanier's mages.

"Zanier, Marcus told me to tell you that we'll be entering Tampa Bay at around six."

Zanier nodded. "Kyle, Tantalus, I've decided on Kyle's plan—he has a point." Fury showed on Tantalus' face. Zanier kept eye contact with him and continued. "Wait till the mercenaries I've hired from Cuba and Brazil arrive in the next few days. We can take on some more risky strategies with them—the loss of their lives is less important to our ultimate goal.

"On another note, I have received word from a RUSA general that he'll sell us armaments much cheaper if what I told him is true and our attack goes as planned—not to mention the sudden need for money in the RUSA vaults."

"You think some connection will be made between us and Alex once we reveal ourselves?" Sara asked calmly.

Zanier said, "If he returns, we won't be able to use him actively in any of our assaults. We'll have to denounce him publicly. Either way, once the New Americans are neutralized, we won't have to worry about that."

Zanier noticed Hannah gulp at the idea of having Alex penned up and unable to help in their work. Sara didn't seem content with the answer.

"When do Kyle and I leave?" Charles said without shifting his view from the map.

"When we enter the bay, you will take a dinghy to shore and head north like we planned. Once there, you will find a man waiting for you with a car. He'll give you the keys and be on his way."

Charles nodded without responding.

"Tantalus, you're wanted to come down and explain the strategy prep to the mages before we start getting ready," Hannah said timidly.

"Yes, of course," Tantalus said, sounding slightly off guard for such a simple question.

This is why you're not in charge! Zanier smiled as they left.

"Promise me that if Alex kills me, you won't put him in charge of the war mages," Kyle said. Though not entirely serious, Sara flinched just the same.

Zanier smiled. "Oh, I wouldn't dare—you two need to prepare as well."

Charles nodded again.

"Yes, sir," Kyle said as he left with Charles.

Zanier stared at Sara—after several seconds, she lowered her gaze and left.

Zanier walked over to the chair by the side of his bed. *Tonight everything changes.*

❋   ❋   ❋

Will and Mike walked across the starboard side of the boat. Land could be seen clearly. Though it appeared that they were parallel to it, they had concluded that they definitely were getting closer.

"This changes things," Will said.

"Yes. We need to find the others."

"Simon is locked up with James, Naomi, and Sam. Karla couldn't stand them anymore so she should be somewhere near the back of the boat."

Mike said, "Hey—I pay attention!"

They made their way to the back of the boat where Karla was leaning over the edge.

"We're getting closer to land," Mike said quickly.

Karla said, "Oh yeah, that makes things easier."

"We're going to find Simon and the others," Will said.

"Okay."

They walked under the deck heading toward their rooms.

"So what's the plan?" Karla asked before Mike knocked on the door.

Simon opened the door and they all entered before Mike answered. "We're going to need to find a way off the boat. I'd say just jump, but we can't with the younger ones."

"What's going on?" Simon asked.

"We're approaching land so were going to make our escape tonight," Will said.

Rolling his eyes, Simon muttered, "We could just ask Hannah."

Mike continued, "All the mages have left to the other boat so this shouldn't be too hard. There are several rescue boats that we've all seen. They're lowered by a pulley system. We can get to one of those and put James, Naomi, Sam, Karla, and Will in, while me and Simon lower it down. Once it's in the water, we can jump."

✱　✱　✱

Alex tried to simply walk around in his search for Molly, but he grew impatient. He hopped to and from shadows—either by teleporting or running cloaked in darkness at all times. Though the sun was high, there were ample shadows from buildings. Sending pulses of dark energy out, he tried to feel for Molly's presence.

After a half hour of searching and four bakeries with no evidence of Molly, he found her. He'd nearly missed her, while moving far too fast and having too much fun. From the top of a house, he saw her talking to a man who looked like a baker. Alex smiled as he realized that the baker was simply nodding and agreeing and that Molly was doing all the talking. Alex quickly teleported into the shadow of the door that had just been opened by a middle-aged woman and he dropped his stealth.

She gasped when he bumped into her, nearly knocking her over. She started cursing under her breath about where the hell he'd come from, but Alex ignored her.

Molly hadn't noticed him so Alex walked up behind her silently. The baker was writing down Molly's suggestions and didn't notice him either. Alex walked right up behind her and said, "So what are you getting me?"

To Alex's amusement, Molly flinched in surprise. Though Alex knew he should have expected it, Molly elbowed him in the gut.

"You couldn't have waited?"

"I was bored. It's not very entertaining in that room all by yourself."

"Well, you could have done something to preoccupy yourself—you're not supposed to go shopping for your own birthday cake."

"I told you I haven't had an actual birthday in a while. I don't know these things."

Molly glared at him to tell him he was full of it. Alex stared back innocently—except for the slight crookedness in his smile. Molly smiled back at Alex before the baker cleared his throat for a question.

"Well umm, this will ..." Alex drowned out the rest of the conversation between them and paced around the bakery. The middle-aged woman critiqued him with her eyes once or twice as she ordered a half-dozen powdered donuts.

Molly walked over to him when he was done. Alex noticed that she was beaming for some reason. "Hey—so how was your walk?"

"Oh good."

"Where did you go?"

"Well, it wasn't really a walk. I went to find Lasorian."

Molly frowned. "Why?"

"I needed to ask him some questions—plus he gave me some very important news."

"What?" Molly's smile started to fade.

"Well, do you remember that Zanier person?"

Her frown sent a twinge of guilt to Alex. "Yeah."

"Well, he's sending two of his best to find me tonight—and I'm going to intercept them before they get too far. I'm doing this tonight."

Molly shrugged and turned around. Before she walked away, she said, "You're going to eat some cake first."

It wasn't the playful tone that Alex was used to—it was almost harsh and definitely demanding. Alex flinched.

CHAPTER 12

Compressed against the side of the boat, Will peered around the corner of the dock to see if anyone was coming. The mages had armed a small group of the crew and told them to keep all the passengers below deck. The rumor among the passengers was that they were going to attack Florida that night. Zanier had returned command of the boat to the captain—as long as he kept all the passengers under control.

They had managed to get onto the deck before the guards could finish setting up. Simon and Karla were trying to figure out how the pulleys worked and Mike was trying to get the boat over the side. James was on watch on the other side. Will saw a guard approaching and fingered his drawn knife. The guard wasn't paying attention to anything more than his cigarette. He stopped and exhaled smoke over the railing. Will was still too small to compete with someone like Alex in a knife fight—or even Mike who was nowhere near as quick as Alex—but Will could throw knives better than anyone he had ever known. He twirled the knife in his fingers, watching the guard carefully. He was armed with a handgun—as they all were.

The guard finished his cigarette and threw it over the side. Turning, he continued to walk in Will's direction. He was going to be able to see him in a moment. Will moved quickly, revealing himself for a better angle, and the knife flew from his fingers. Before the guard knew what had happened, he fell to the ground with the knife through his skull. Will quickly ran to him, retrieved his knife, and dragged the man overboard. Cursing at the bloodstains, he ran back to the corner. There was a guard close behind, but it would be some time before he got to the bloodstains.

Wiping the majority of the blood off his knife on the side of the boat, he decided he needed to warn Mike and Simon. Surprised and suddenly nervous, Will heard James yell out to him when he rounded the corner.

"There are guards coming this way," Simon said.

"James just told us the same thing," Karla answered.

"Have you guys figured this out yet?"

"Yeah—they just need to get it over the edge," Karla answered. James looked nervously in the guard's direction.

"How far is he, James?"

"He'll be able to see us soon."

"Watch my side—I'll be back."

Will hadn't expected James to actually fight anyone— yet. He was a good thief, but he was still young and hesitated to use a knife in a fight. Will couldn't remember being afraid to kill. Knife in hand, Will moved quickly along the wall. The guard was armed with his handgun holstered. This was as close as he could get to the guard without being seen. Will wasn't confident that he could hit the guard's head so he aimed at the man's chest. The knife flew from his hand, but the guard saw him a moment before the knife hit his chest. It must have missed the heart because the guard was able to draw his gun. Will hugged the wall as the guard fired at where he thought he was. Will cursed at the noise. Soon the gunshots ceased and Will looked around the corner again. The man had bled out and no one was in sight. Will retrieved his knife, wiping the blood off on the man's pants. A shotgun blast forced Will to the ground. Three more guards were on the way and they had shotguns instead of pistols. Will set off back toward his friends at full tilt before they could fire again.

"Hurry—they're coming! Has James come back?"

"Not yet," Mike answered. They had the boat over the edge and everyone except for Simon and Mike were inside.

"Start lowering it. I'm getting him. There are three men behind me," Mike said as he and Simon started lowering the boat.

A guard aimed his pistol at James, but Will let a knife fly before the man could see him. James jumped as the man fell over limply.

"Hurry—we have to go!" James turned and ran after Will.

The boat was almost in the water. Mike and Simon were still working the pulley. The three guards were moving toward them and shouting. Will grabbed James and, lifting him up, shouted toward Mike and Simon before he swung over the railing.

❋   ❋   ❋

Molly watched Alex put on the solid black bulletproof suit he'd worn when he robbed Fort Knox. Grabbing his cape, he swung it over his back. Molly sat cross-legged on the bed facing Alex's back. In front of her was the cake. It had been a very good layer cake—chocolate with strawberry frosting and chunks of strawberries.

They'd managed to eat a good chunk of it, but still more than half remained. Molly had been rather desperately hoping this moment wouldn't come since Alex had told her what he had to do. They'd had a good time earlier, but it hadn't been quite what she'd hoped for. Alex was always not entirely there—though he'd laugh and joke with her, his eyes were always distant.

Unable to stand the silence anymore Molly asked, "Will you see her?"

"Who?" Alex asked.

"Hannah."

Alex turned to face Molly.

"I don't think so. I'm not going to be that close to Tampa."

Molly noticed Alex struggling with a buckle on his left side. She got up and helped him buckle it.

"Thanks."

Molly lingered at Alex's side. His presence was hypnotizing and his breath dazed her. Alex started to move, but Molly didn't want him leave. He picked up his gloves, sword belt, and sheath. Molly hardly noticed him leave through door.

Putting the cake in the fridge, she fell into bed in a heap of emotions.

❋   ❋   ❋

The clock in Zanier's room read 5:48. Leaving his room, he headed to the top deck.

❋   ❋   ❋

Charles was solemn and depressed as he drove.

"What's up? You don't look too excited."

"Should I be?"

"Well," Kyle said. "We're off that boat for once."

"And?"

"It was getting kind of boring. At least now we get to stretch our legs out a bit more."

"If you consider long car rides across this war-ravaged country in search of a rogue shadow caster stretching your legs, well, you enjoy."

"Yeah, sorry for being optimistic. I've been getting enough depressing talks from Sara."

"She at least acknowledges that Alex might pose more of a threat than Zanier is willing to admit. Maybe you should listen to her."

"I do. I know quite well what Alex can do. I've taken the brunt of most of his overuses or uncontrolled uses of power."

Charles was silent and Kyle gave up trying to get him to talk.

※　※　※

They'd anchored the other boat in the middle of the bay. Hannah was part of the left flank of their assault. Tantalus had arranged them into their three groups. The healers would follow them and supply support from behind. Zanier would provide a massive shield around them.

Tantalus paced at the head of the ship in front of the guardians he'd led into battle. Two patrol boats demanded that they state their business and supply them with identification. The second one was bigger than the first and had armed personnel on it—both had ample heavy artillery. Tantalus seemed irritated by the boats.

They were far into the bay when a third patrol boat replaced the first. When they threatened to open fire, Tantalus smiled. Tantalus never gave them the chance to make good on their threat. Standing in the front of the boat, he held out both hands toward the boats. Without even looking at them, two bus-sized fireballs erupted from his hands. The boats exploded simultaneously.

Sirens went up along the entire bay as both patrol boats sank, smoldering. The guardian mages instantly raised a barrier around the boat as machine gun fire and turrets from the shore collided into it. Other boats were being launched, but Tantalus sent wave after wave of fireballs at them. Hannah was amazed that he didn't even allow the other war mages to help him. *Fool! He'll have nothing left when we land.* Tantalus stood strong. Light from the setting sun turning his hair as red as the fire that erupted from his hands.

※　※　※

Alex stood atop the tallest building he could find in Jacksonville and gazed at the setting sun. He'd tired himself out getting there so fast. He needed to get Kyle and Charles' attention. He had a plan for it, but he'd need more power. Staring at the setting sun, he began his wait.

※　※　※

The boat reached as far as it could into the bay. Troops had marshaled on the shore. Huge amounts of firepower poured down onto the shield that the guardians held with ease.

Hannah felt the adrenaline pump through her as she and all the other mages leapt from the boat. As one unit of grace and destruction, the mages glided through the air, unleashing wave after wave of magic energy. No attack was the same in form or color. As Tantalus released massive balls of fire, Hannah's strikes were like pale gold lightning.

The rush of power was amazing; Hannah had never felt more alive. Leading the left wing of the assault, she rushed into a fortified position protected by her shield and those that overlapped her. The gunner at the turret died first as her arcane lightning lifted him off the ground. Before she attacked again, strikes from other mages leveled the position. Almost surprised, Hannah was swept back into the mass of war mages.

❊　❊　❊

The sun was beginning to drop behind the horizon and Alex could feel the power of that which was coming. Drawing ever so cautiously from shadows around him, he sent a pulse of power over several miles to detect Kyle and Charles. He found them heading up a road several miles to the southwest. In a second, he was airborne. He constantly sent out pulses of power to keep track of where they were.

Just a few miles north, Alex hid in the shadow of a bridge that crossed the highway. *No need for attention yet*. He could see their car just a few hundred yards south moving a bit faster than the rest of the traffic. They were separated from the closest cars and were about to go under the bridge. Alex jumped, dropping his stealth. Instantly he heard brakes and the car swerved. Reaching out with his powers, he grabbed its shadow, holding steady and preventing its collision course with a pillar.

Horns blared and concerned pedestrians ran out of their cars to stop traffic. Shaken, but very much alive, with shields surrounding them, Kyle and Charles crawled out of the car.

"Alex?" Charles said.

"You wanted to find me?" Alex answered.

"Not here," Kyle said.

"Why not?" Alex answered again.

Kyle shrugged. A crowd was forming. The green robes of Kyle and Charles and the solid black suit and cape of Alex caused hesitation.

"We were sent to take you back," Charles said bluntly.

"I know."

"So what is it? Are you coming or not?" Kyle said.

"I am not going with you," Alex said calmly.

"Sorry, Alex. You give us no choice," Kyle said before sending a stun pulse at him. Almost embarrassed by the attack, Alex deflected it.

"You'll have to do better than that," Alex said. He drew rapidly on the surrounding darkness and the coming night. People screamed as shadows seemed to cling to Alex.

❋   ❋   ❋

Kyle, shocked by the sudden display of power, raised a shield around himself. Charles had done the same. Soon enough, Charles would be shielding both of them so Kyle would be doing all the attacking. *What was he doing?* He thought that Alex was attacking them, but it looked as if he was manipulating the darkness to cling to him. *What a waste of power.* Then he took off into the air. *More wasted power.* He sent several quick pulses of pale blue lightning at Alex, but he easily maneuvered around them.

In a second, he was out of range.

"Damn it!" Charles said. "Now we have to chase him, we're going to be wasting power twice as fast as him in the air."

Without responding, he took off after Alex.

❄   ❄   ❄

Alex weaved skillfully around Kyle's strikes. He flew away from them—careful to keep them just in range—and soon they were over a small city. Alex hadn't planned for an aerial battle over a city.

The sun was completely gone now and it was almost perfectly dark—except for the stars and the city below. The moon wasn't very high in the sky. Drawing more and more power around him, he started to return fire at Kyle. His attacks were deflected off of a constant shield that he now noticed was being held by Charles. Switching targets, he went for Charles. Not sending anything overly powerful at him, he tried to constantly draw power from the night since it was slower than using his natural store.

Alex kept trying to position himself so that Charles blocked him from Kyle's view, forcing him to be less accurate with his attacks. Unexpectedly, Charles sent a fairly powerful pulse of power that looked like a flat blade of white fire. The blast slammed into Alex's fairly weak shield. Alex focused more power into his shield as Kyle hit him with two consecutive bolts.

With all his power in his shield, Alex began to fall. Alex reached out, trying to draw more and more power. Air rushed by as he plunged closer and closer to the ground. Kyle and Charles were right behind him now. His cape was nearly plastered to his body by the wind as he angled himself toward the ground. With a massive force of energy, Alex switched direction not two feet from the ground. He rocketed along a road—weaving around unsuspecting cars and screaming pedestrians. Before the road forked around a church, Alex hurtled himself into the air, grasping for more and more power.

Alex felt a sudden chill shudder through him as he felt more power swarm into him. It was violent and much quicker than ever before. A feeling of ecstasy shot through him and he couldn't help smiling. Kyle and Charles were not a hundred feet behind him. Without even thinking, Alex sent a massive continuous stream of power through his left hand at Charles. He was stopped dead as he raised his shields. Kyle swung around to Alex's right and started sending many rapid bolts at him. Alex raised his right hand and created a shield. It wasn't even difficult. Alex felt the power pulse through him as he gathered more and more. He had now gathered all the power he needed, but he couldn't stop gathering more—far more—than he needed. He couldn't stop it—it felt too good.

"Alex, stop this!"

Alex noticed Charles gradually sinking in the air. Alex couldn't understand the horror in Kyle's eyes. Fear ripped through him as he realized that he was no longer in control.

"He's almost out of power—you're going to kill him. How are you doing this?"

Alex stopped sending energy at Charles. Kyle seemed to be relieved for a second. Alex was confused and then he felt his power rearranging. He still wasn't in control and Alex couldn't figure out what it was doing. Alex stared at Charles—horrified and unable to control himself, but knowing far too vividly what he was about to do. He met

Charles' gaze and darkness surrounded him. *I can avoid his shields. That's what my power was doing. No! I can't!* Alex felt his left hand raise palm up. The darkness around Charles thickened and organized. Regaining some control of his body, he felt himself tremble. Kyle must have noticed something was wrong because he renewed his attacks. Alex could have sworn that he was yelling too, but his focus was elsewhere. He tried to regain control, but he was terrified. He had no idea how to stop himself. Charles' eyes glazed in horror—he seemed to hear all of Alex's thoughts.

Alex closed his hand and willed the darkness to avoid Charles' shield.

❋   ❋   ❋

Kyle watched helplessly as Alex's dark power ripped through his defenseless friend. Charles' shield was doing nothing.

His throat was raw from shouting. Alex seemed to hover in place as horrified as Kyle was.

"No!" Kyle dove after Charles' falling lifeless body. Alex was quicker and he caught it right before it clipped the side of a building. He continued descending till he landed on the road with the body.

Kyle landed beside him and noticed that Alex's eyes were glazed over.

Alex's voice quivered as he said, "I lost control … I … I couldn't … too much power. It knew how to avoid his shields."

Kyle approached slowly and reached out to take Charles.

"No!" Kyle suddenly was afraid that Alex had lost control again. "I'll take him—and you too. I can bring you there in a matter of seconds—and you can't."

*   *   *

Hannah's mind was numb as she gazed across the city. She couldn't quite remember the sweep of the city. Her attacks had torn into soldiers and buildings as the attack persisted. It had been easy—there was no challenge to it. It felt good to be so strong and to no longer feel fear.

It was then that Zanier's voice rocked the city. "The New Americans are retreating. Let them run. Create defensive positions around the city. Citizens of Tampa, we have liberated you from these false leaders. We offer you to join us. I am Zanier and these are my mages. We are here to cleanse this war-torn country and to bring it back to its former glory. We come wielding long-forgotten powers that some of you may even be able to use. Come to the bay and we will test you. If you can wield the power of magic, we will unlock your potential and we will train you in the uses of your power. If this gift is not yours, you may still feel free to join us. Swear loyalty to us and you will thus forth be under our protection."

Zanier's magically amplified voice woke Hannah from her trance. As she headed back to the boat, she was shocked at exactly how much damage had been dealt.

*   *   *

Simon and Mike climbed soaking wet into the small rescue boat. Will lounged comfortably on the inflated edge. James sat calmly two feet away from him while Karla comforted Sam and Naomi.

Simon wrapped himself in a blanket on the floor while Mike cranked the engine to life. Seconds later, the boat was speeding toward land. Will enjoyed the light spray as he peered deeper into the bay. The explosions had begun moments after leaping off the boat and were now happening across the city. Mages were moving quickly; apparently none of the city's defenses were able to slow them down. Will wondered what the mages were going to do.

A hundred yards from shore, Will could see what looked like a movie in the streets of Tampa. All sorts of things flew out of green-robed people's hands. Mike cut the engine as they ran ashore. Will hesitated to leave and waited until everyone except Mike and Simon were off the boat.

"We have to push it out," Will said.

"What?"

"If they find it, they'll know where we are."

"It'll just drift back sooner or later."

"I've got an idea."

"Stop," Mike said.

Without listening, Will twisted the boat around so that it faced out to sea. He jumped in near the engine and brought it to life.

"Wait."

Still ignoring Mike, Will jumped out and let the boat zoom aimlessly into the dark.

"What the hell was that for?"

"Just in case the mages look for us."

Karla walked up behind Mike and wrapped her arms around his waist, calming him instantly.

Mike shrugged before speaking. "Let's find a place to rest."

✳   ✳   ✳

Alex leaned heavily on the door to the apartment. He couldn't enter—not with the memories still burning hot in his head and painfully scalding his mind.

Hannah's gaze was almost as painful as seeing her in green robes. Charles' body was still in his arms and Kyle was at his side, overtaking him as Alex slowed. Zanier's attention shifted toward him. Sara gasped in pain and fear. The other healers rushed to the motionless body as Alex laid it on the ground.

"Alex, what have you done?" Zanier said.

"Alex?" Hannah's voice was not so well controlled.

Kyle approached Sara slowly as she ran to embrace him.

"He's dead," one of the younger healers said.

"Alex?" Hannah repeated. "You killed him—didn't you? Why?"

"His powers," Zanier said. "He is not in control."

"I am now," Alex said. "You forced my hand, you made me fight—"

"I gave you a choice—"

"You already knew the answer!" Alex was almost surprised at the strength of his voice. "I can't be defeated by any mere mage—even you!"

"How dare you!" Zanier's yelled.

"Me? All the power of darkness is mine! I am the shadow caster! I am the master of all the darkness in the universe!"

Hannah spoke, "Alex, please. Please come back—we need you."

"You do not. It seems you did quite well here today. Zanier, do not search for me again. I cannot promise that I won't lose control again—or maybe I won't lose control at all." Alex tried to smile to get his message across—and it seemed to work.

It would have worked better if Hannah hadn't grabbed his hand. She said, "Alex, with you we can end this war."

Alex said, "I will find a way to end this, but I will not conquer the world in order to free it!" His voice grew fierce as he directed his eyes at Zanier. He stared down Zanier for several moments before teleporting.

Alex turned the door handle and stumbled into the room. Almost able to maintain balance, he fell into something warm that hung onto him.

"Alex! What happened?"

"Molly?" Alex surrendered his weight to her. He put his head on her shoulder as he slipped willingly into unconsciousness.

Chapter 13

Molly stroked a strand of Alex's hair out of his face. He'd been in bed all night and well into the morning. She had removed his jumpsuit and cape and made sure that he wasn't injured.

The horrible sense of weakness and helplessness had dulled only slightly. She looked over Alex's sleeping figure as she'd been doing almost the entire night. *What happened? What should I do?* She couldn't stand that Alex had gone out to defend not only himself—but her as well. She had done nothing.

Absentmindedly she ran her hand down the side of his body, hesitating around his yellowish bruises. His body was firm with muscle, but he'd not quite outgrown the slenderness of youth. *He's only seventeen. How many had he killed?—and his own father. What had he done last night? Could he have added more to that count? Did he kill any of Zanier's mages? Did they force him back? Could they teleport too? If he lost, would they find him?* The many questions made her feel useless.

She moved slightly closer. He always appeared so strong and confident when he was awake. However, when he was sleeping soundly, he was vulnerable.

Moving closer, her hand now held the side of his head. Lightly leaning into him, she kissed him—only for a second before she pulled away. Alex shifted slightly. Molly's heart skipped a beat, but he continued to sleep motionlessly.

Rolling away from him, she faced the other wall. *What was that? Idiot! There's that other girl—I can't do this.* Hating herself more than before, Molly stormed out of the apartment. Hesitating for a second and looking at Alex, she took her sunglasses and left.

Determined not to be useless again, she headed for the woods. Lasorian would help her—he'd train her. She remembered all too clearly the speech he'd given Alex. Not all spell casters had to be gifted—there were other ways to gain power. Determination flowing through her, she entered the woods.

❋   ❋   ❋

Zanier's words meant nothing to him as he looked around a circle dominated by green robes. In the center of the circle was the pyre where Charles' body rested. They had no time to bury him so Zanier created a new tradition. He proclaimed that every mage who died would be cremated to release all of his remaining power.

The priest had been one of the first to approach Zanier and the first to be proclaimed as gifted. He was a healer, which seemed to suit him well. He'd been trying to help the poor here for as long as the New Americans had been in control. Shifting his gaze, Zanier continued around the circle to Sara and Kyle. Sara had only released Kyle from her grip for the few seconds he'd needed to talk. Retelling the events of the night before hadn't helped him. The part that had most startled him was not Alex's loss of control, but the limitlessness to his power; the intense aerial battle Kyle had described held little interest to Zanier but Alex seemingly pulling darkness towards himself did. He'd have to do some research on that.

His gaze continued from Kyle to Sara. She buried her head into his robes. Her eyes were filled with twisted relief crossed with fear. Zanier guessed that she was picturing Kyle in Charles' place.

Hannah. Zanier couldn't tell who Hannah was sad for— perhaps she mourned Charles. She'd been oblivious to his truly sinister side—part of his and Zanier's ploy to make her belong more to the mages than to Alex. Most likely it was for her loss of Alex knowing that he wasn't going to return to the mages. He looked her over more thoroughly. He hadn't bothered to notice earlier, but she was quite an attractive girl. The robe brought out the green in her eyes. A large number of the younger male mages were looking at her rather than the pyre. *I better pay attention. I wonder how many of them would like to comfort her.*

The preacher had finished and was now looking at Zanier. Closing his eyes, Zanier took in a deep breath. Raising his hands and releasing his breath, he willed fire to the pyre. No simple fire, but a large inferno. He surrounded it with a shield so no heat would escape. It was good for the mages to be reminded how powerful he was. Lowering his hands not five seconds after he lit the blaze, he looked around the circle again. Many of the weaker or newer mages were looking at him now instead of the pyre, which was now not much more than ashes.

With the ceremony done, Zanier left. Today would not be a day for rest. The mercenaries had arrived and were awaiting his command. They were going to divide into two forces. One would head east and the other south. Their job would be to clear out the rest of the panhandle while the mages pushed north. Tampa provided seven new mages, three healers, a war mage, and three guardians. Tomorrow's shipment of armaments would allow Zanier to start forming a regular army. It would also arm the weaker mages so they didn't have to waste power with attacks. Zanier smiled as the leader of the mercenaries approached.

✳   ✳   ✳

Molly hesitated for a second, thinking that she'd gone the wrong way when a strong smell of incense hit her. In the last few yards before the clearing, it became almost intoxicating. Approaching the clearing, she saw Lasorian standing at its center. A formless cloud of mist hovered over what appeared to be a metal fire pit. In one hand, he held a bag from which he threw things into a pot while chanting illegibly.

Approaching slowly, Molly got a better look at the pot. In the center of the mist, a more solid object cast ghostly lights. Its shape was almost circular, but it constantly seemed to change size and dimensions.

Though almost noon, the only source of light in the clearing seemed to be the object in the mist. Molly wanted to see the sky, but she couldn't take her eyes off of the spectacle. Lasorian's voice started to rise and the pace of his chanting increased. The object seemed to react, shifting forms much quicker than before. As quickly as the pace had changed, Lasorian stopped completely. He bent his head forward slightly and—for a second that felt like an eternity—the mist swirled even faster than before till they were seemingly sucked into it. Another impossibly long second passed before it imploded; the shock wave knocked Molly off her feet.

Awaking from her trance, Molly tried to stand, but it was difficult to gain balance. Once on her feet, Molly looked at where the mist and the object had been. Lasorian and the pit was all that was left. He put a small blue marble in his bag.

"To what do I owe your company?" Lasorian asked.

"What was that?"

"I was scrying."

"Scrying?"

"I was looking into the whereabouts of certain people. I deviated a little at the end, trying to see some events to come."

"You can tell the future?"

"Limited—and as you saw, it's a very volatile process."

"Oh."

"This is not why you came."

"Umm ... yeah." Molly felt suddenly nervous. "I ... I want to become a warlock."

"*Witch* you mean," he said. "It's been a while since I last trained someone."

"What do I need to do?"

"That's up to you. I can't help you till you've chosen a demon to bind yourself to—and you have performed the ritual."

"Okay. What do I need to do that?"

"Not much. Some chalk and this book will do." He pulled a book from an unseen pocket and handed it to Molly. "Be sure that your shadow caster doesn't get too much information. I doubt he'll be too keen about the demon thing."

"My shadow caster? You can see the future—what have you seen?"

"My dear, that is like reading the last chapter of the book instead of enjoying the whole thing."

Molly went to call after him, but thought better of it. Smiling to herself, she turned and left.

✳ ✳ ✳

Alex heard a door shut. He tried to drift back to sleep, but his body refused. In rebellion against himself, he shut his eyes again. Something warm brushed against his head, moving his hair out of his face.

"Come on—wake up. I saw you move." The voice was familiar and warm. He was almost compelled to obey.

There was silence for a few seconds before Alex felt an impact on the other side of the bed. Opening his eyes, he saw Molly's face surprisingly close.

"Hey," she said smoothly. Alex hadn't truly looked into her eyes before. They were deep brown and almost hypnotizing. "What happened last night?"

The words brought back a pain that he didn't want to face.

"Well, I'm gonna find out one way or another."

"I fought them. I lost control. I tried for too much power. I couldn't control it. I killed Charles. His shields were useless. My power did something, but I couldn't tell what."

There was some excitement in Molly's eyes. *Why can't she hate me now?* Curious, Alex sent out a slight pulse of power. She radiated excitement and something else that Alex could not quite define.

"And?" Alex hadn't realized how long he'd been staring at her.

"I caught him before he hit that building. Kyle ... I don't really know what Kyle was thinking—and I don't think I want to. The way he looked at me—I brought him back. I tried acting strong to intimidate Zanier so he wouldn't send anyone after me—us. I think it worked—and then there was Hannah."

"What?" The look in Hannah's eyes hurt more than anything else did.

"She was horrified, I think. She tried to get me to stay. I think I hurt her. The way she looked at me—I almost failed. I almost lost control of my emotions when she touched my hand." Alex instantly regretted saying so much. Something about Molly's eyes had changed.

Alex suddenly felt self-conscious. He couldn't bear to look into her eyes anymore. She made him feel guilty somehow—looking at her shouldn't make him feel good.

Alex sighed as he rolled to the other side of the bed. He got up and started digging through the drawers for clothes. Molly laughed at his awkwardness as he got into clothes.

"Oh, so you can't talk to me anymore." Her voice was flirty and smooth—with a slight hint of longing.

By the time he had a shirt and shorts on, he heard steps coming closer behind him.

"You know—you don't look half bad in boxers." He hadn't realized how close she had gotten. Molly's warm hand caressed his neck. He felt electricity flow through him and then her breath on the back of his neck.

Her other hand wrapped around his neck. Her eyes were fierce with a fire that had been hidden before. Slowly, she leaned closer to him and pulled herself closer. Alex couldn't resist. He closed the distance and their lips met. Her lips were soft and her mouth was wet. Alex ran his hands down her back and pulled her closer. She felt so good, so warm, and so full of life. *Why do I feel so guilty?* It was as if she had read his mind. Feeling him holding back, she committed all her weight into him. Alex lost balance when the back of his legs hit the dresser. Alex fell to the floor with Molly on top of him.

Alex wasn't sure if he was smiling. *No, yes, no, yes, no! Yes!* Molly wrapped her hands around his head and went to kiss him again. Alex ran his hands through her hair. The guilt was too much—he couldn't do this.

"No," Alex said.

Molly seemed to ignore him, but he started pushing her off. "No, please."

"What?"

She sat back onto her knees.

"I can't."

"Why not?"

Alex couldn't think of an answer. Her hair was messed up and her eyes held a different type of fire. She truly was beautiful. *That isn't helping.*

"What is it? Hannah? She's with Zanier now. Why didn't she come with you? You can't go to her now—can you?"

"I'm sorry." Alex didn't feel any better, but his guilt was replaced by another.

Molly screamed, "Sorry? Sorry for what? You're so pathetic!"

❋   ❋   ❋

Molly couldn't understand him. She wanted to hit him—to do something—just to make him snap out of this.

Alex couldn't bear Molly's glare. Looking briefly into her eyes—he felt that by even existing, he was hurting her. He walked by her as she kneeled on the floor. Not even bothering to open the door, Alex was gone.

CHAPTER 14

Alex watched the TV and felt utterly useless. A week had passed since Zanier's invasion had begun. Their unexplainable abilities were still being described as some new technology that the RUSA was supposedly researching. The word magic was utterly taboo in the news, but people were talking. The RUSA news stations were also considering the mages as their long-awaited ally in the war against the New Americans. All of Florida was Zanier's and he hadn't stopped there—he had moved into Georgia. Alex guessed that Zanier's next attack point would be Savannah.

He would stop Zanier there. He knew what Zanier wanted. He wasn't going to stop till he had complete domain over all of the former USA. Alex didn't disagree with Zanier ending the war—he just didn't like how Zanier was going about it. He would be the ruler and his word law—for no other reason than he was the strongest.

Alex hadn't spent the previous week dormant. He had been training rigorously every single night and trying to push himself to the point of loss of control. Only once could he not recover. All he had done was horribly disfigure several acres of wilderness. He'd found a way to sustain himself by constantly drawing on power. He had gone almost three days without rest or food and had not felt tired or hungry. He hadn't wanted to return to the room after what had happened with Molly. She had been worried and didn't think it was right not to rest. She'd also been up to something. Every time he entered the room, she acted as if she'd been doing something wrong. One time, he caught her trying to hide something, but he never brought it up. *Better not to be involved with anything she does.*

He had a good idea the next night. Zanier would move, but he had other business to take care of first. The New American senate was meeting and Alex intended to be there. He'd tell them of his plan to stop Zanier and reveal to them the world that they—as well as the RUSA—were oblivious to. *It's about time this denial stopped and they knew what they were dealing with.* Already dressed in his black suit, he soared into the air. He needed to see Molly first—she deserved to know what he was doing.

❋   ❋   ❋

Molly ran her finger along the page of Lasorian's book, converting the words to memory. *Succubus.* The upper part of the page was dominated by a picture of a beautiful female demon with a description below.

> *This seductive female demon is among one of the most feared across the mortal plane. Its name—though many times misused—has been linked to whores, alleged prostitutes, or seductresses for seducing husbands and lovers. Through its straight power, it uses fire to emulate its enemies—preferring the slow, more painful means of dealing death after it has caught its opponent off guard.*

The description continued, but Molly had already read it multiple times. This was the demon she wanted to bind and she'd gone over its ritual many times. Of all the demons, its side effects to the binder were much more bearable. Its ritual—by no means easy—required very little supplies. A strong incense and red chalk for the inscriptions around the circles and white chalk for the circles. There would be eight circles in the ritual: two overlapping inner ones for Molly and the demon and six surrounding ones for the six lesser demons she'd summon first. Those souls would act to strengthen the inner two circles and would combine with the demons before ultimately binding to Molly.

Molly heard steps outside the door. She shoved her bookmark in and slid the book under the bed seconds before Alex entered. Alex hardly used the door anymore. Dark circles had formed under his eyes and he somehow managed to look thinner. Molly had been against Alex trying to sustain himself only on the shadows.

"Alex! Have you lost your mind? You can't be serious!" Molly yelled.

"It's fine," he answered calmly—as if he wasn't all there.

"Why are you doing this to yourself? You're not eating either!"

"I need more time."

"Time! You train at night. You could at least sleep during the day—and for god's sake, Alex, eat something!"

"During the day, I need to keep practicing drawing power from the shadows. It's harder during the day than at night—and there isn't nearly as much to use."

"God damn you! You're not helping yourself! Alex, you're not eating at all, are you?"

＊　＊　＊

Alex crossed the room like a ghost leaning against the wall. *He looks so tired so . . . dead.*

"What?" Molly stared at him, not bothering to hide the pitiful tone to her voice.

"Tonight I'm going to the New American senate. I'm going to tell them about everything and my plan to stop Zanier at Savannah." He spoke like he was talking to himself.

Molly nodded in response.

"You've been up to something—I know you have. Please don't lie to me—I can detect your surface emotions and sometimes thoughts."

Can he? That's new—maybe that's why he doesn't look at me.
"Why?"

His look was enough to interrupt her. "Molly, please."

"Why should I tell you? All I want to do is help and you can't even let me do that. Alex, look at yourself!"

His eyes drooped in a shrug. His hair fell in front of his face. The blackness of his suit and his hair contrasted against his skin, which had gotten drastically paler since he started moving in the shadows and training at night. His high cheekbones were more pronounced against his skeletal face. The darkness had sustained him enough so that he hadn't visibly lost any muscle mass. He was truly a sight—enough to make his power believable to almost anyone.

"Alex, you don't have to do this. I . . ."

Love you, holy shit!

"Alex, you don't have to do this alone. You don't have to be alone."

"Molly, what have you done?"

He almost looked human again—his eyes pleaded.

"Nothing yet—and you won't stop me either."

"Molly …"

"I thought you were going."

Molly felt as if something had horribly malfunctioned in her heart when he vanished in a mist of darkness.

✳   ✳   ✳

Alex felt power surge to him as he rocketed toward Washington. Moving at speeds that would tear a normal human to shreds, he kept a constant shield around himself and kept himself invisible.

Alex watched as he passed from RUSA to New America. The distinction was almost startling. Ghettos were everywhere. It was like watching flowering fields suddenly become an industrialized and CO_2-chocked Sahara Desert—minus the sand. *Why am I helping these people?* Alex knew he wasn't actually helping them—he was helping inform them about what was truly happening. Looking at the poor place he had lived two months ago, he wasn't entirely sure that he wanted to stop Zanier. There was no guarantee that Zanier would help them—and there definitely was a guarantee that Zanier would be the law.

The buildings grew nicer as he approached DC. Alex cut speed and drifted over the White House. It had been a while since a president had lived there. The senate ran everything now and three high senators were in charge of that with two-thirds of the vote in their hands. The senate building wasn't too hard to find. It was surrounded by cars and people—not to mention absolutely ridiculous amounts of security. Alex, still cloaked in darkness, dove toward a window and teleported into a guard's shadow.

The guard stood motionlessly and did not notice Alex. Alex moved to the railing. The meeting had already begun and a lady was speaking. Alex recognized her as the senator whose charisma had started the whole civil war. Late in middle age, her voice was a little raspy and her skin had started to dull and wrinkle. Her hair was cropped short and was blondish-gray.

"Senator Richard and Senator Rivera are responsible for the events of the past week. They have irresponsibly spent their funds, leaving the state of Florida's defenses in a state of disrepair."

"What funds?" Rivera asked. "We can hardly keep our fire departments and emergency services going. How can you expect that we'd be able to mount a sufficient defense?"

"Due to your failure …"

"Failure? You are what has failed!"

"How dare you bring allegations against High Senator Mullen?" A young lanky male senator rose from across the room.

"I dismiss you from this senate!" Senator Mullen yelled.

"A vote, Miss Mullen," an elderly senator said. The title seemed to cause her to flinch. She turned to face the senator. "High Senator Mullen, not Miss! Or has old age rattled your brains, High Senator Hunter?" The older senator had a full head of gray hair and a well-kept beard. He was also strikingly tall—maybe six and half feet.

"No, *High Senator* Mullen, my brain hasn't slowed a bit. As for yours …" He smiled, not finishing the thought. "You may wish to cease these allegations and allow us to get somewhere in this meeting so that we can appropriately deal with the issues at hand."

Alex was quite interested in the debate, but decided to make his appearance. Selecting the lights around the edges of the room, Alex gripped them with power and shattered them, leaving only a small cluster in the center. Now that the room was darker, Alex had no trouble reaching outside for power. He teleported behind the senators and let an aura of darkness surround him as he rose from the kneeling position he'd landed in. Focusing on the energy in the room, he drained it. Lowering the temperature of the room was a nice trick he'd learned that week.

Everyone was looking at him—some too shocked to look afraid—all but one didn't really surprise him. It must be instinct for her to condemn people.

"Kill him—kill the intruder!" *Come on. You can be a bit more creative.*

Bullets uselessly bounced off Alex's shield. Alex reached out and focused on the power around him. He flexed his will and the bullets stopped for just a second—long enough for the brain to realize what had just happened. They reversed direction—some were lethal and some only hurt the guards. Most ricocheted off gun barrels. Alex didn't care—it was enough to make them stop firing.

"I don't want to, but it'd be all too easy to kill all of you."

Alex smiled slyly as he stepped forward.

"And what do think you're doing making these threats!" Mullen yelled at Alex. It was a statement more than a question, but Alex decided to treat it as a question.

He reached out and darkness thickened around her throat. Focusing his magic within her throat, he thickened it. For a moment, she couldn't breathe. She clawed at her throat and fell to her knees. Alex aligned his power around her throat so that air could pass through, but no sound would come out.

Alex swept his gaze across the room—everyone was silent. Alex didn't know what to feel about how they looked at him. Their fear almost made him feel guilty, but it was invigorating to have them all under his will.

"Tomorrow, Zanier will attack Savannah," Alex said calmly. "He leads an army of mages. They wield magic as their weapons and there are enough to get through without being bothered by your useless modern defenses.

"I will be there tomorrow and I will stop them. I can use the most powerful form of magic in history. I can control all the darkness and the dark negative energies in the world. I can also draw power from the shadows and my power is next to limitless at night."

He let this sit for a while as the senators tried to comprehend him. The older high senator was the first to speak.

"Magic?"

"Yes."

"Explain."

Alex smiled. "The story of magic is long. I just know a little—and even that would keep us here for a while." Alex took a long breath before repeating Lasorian's story. The faces of the senators ranged from utter defiance to complete confusion.

"Liar!" Mullen's previous supporter had regained his voice, while she glared at Alex. Composure wasn't all she'd recovered. She pointed a handgun at Alex.

"Leave now!" her supporter yelled and she nodded.

Alex reached out and released a pulse of dark energy. It struck the gun and seemed to almost explode in her hands.

The shock of the blast threw her back fifteen feet into a desk. She coughed—broken, but still very much alive.

"So, what is it you wish for us to do?" said a Native American senator.

"Nothing for now. This isn't helping anyone. I'm here to stop Zanier. If I fail, then worry about him. If I were you, I'd start learning how you can govern your country. RUSA is in no position to fight anyone right now—so you have time."

Alex called the darkness and vanished into nothing.

✳ ✳ ✳

Alex approached the door to the room. He was truly exhausted—not physically, he could keep himself going indefinitely—but he needed the escape of a long sleep. He felt a strong smell and it took a second before he realized that it was coming from his room. *What is she doing?* Alex went to teleport, picking a shadow he'd always used. It didn't work. *What the hell? Does she think she can keep me out?* He looked the door over and grabbed at its shadow. He tried to bend it, but it didn't move. He shipped out his long knife, focusing on the small gap between the door and the building. He used his power to guide his swing and to amplify the power. He struck the deadbolt and it gave. The normal lock went with a little less grace. When the door swung open, he saw that the bed—and everything else—had been pushed aside. The carpet had been rolled up and there were more lights than Alex had ever seen in a place that small. They were all spread out, removing any shadow that Alex might have used.

Molly was horrified to see Alex standing completely confused. She finished the final circle and jumped into one of the overlapping circles. Lasorian's book was still in her hands.

"What are you doing?"

Molly started the ritual. Her voice had strangeness to it and the words that came from mouth held a power that they'd never had before.

Chapter 15

Alex tried to walk toward Molly, but couldn't. At the very edge of the circles and inscriptions she'd drawn, Alex ran into a barrier. It was as physical as it was mental. Drawing on power, Alex assaulted the wall. Dark energy whipped around, bouncing out of control and ricocheting off the walls. Several lights went off and Alex watched Molly wince. Her voice sounded slightly weak. Alex stopped and Molly's voice returned to normal. *Damn it! I'm hurting her.*

"Molly?" Alex paced around the circle behind Molly.

She continued speaking in low indiscernible syllables until Alex completed a lap.

"Alex, please. This is dangerous. I'm protected by the inscriptions and circles—please leave."

"I don't think I'm the one who needs to be worried about." He sent out pulses of energy at various lights, shattering them and darkening the room slightly before shutting the door. *No need for anyone else to see this.*

"Now tell me what you're doing."

"I'm becoming a warlock ... I mean a witch."

"What?"

"It's what I want, Alex. I'm going to do it so just shut up and watch—and why the hell didn't you just turn off the lights?"

Alex sulked into the corner of the room. Molly had already begun the ritual again and wasn't stopping. Small fires rose from the incense in the six surrounding circles and slowly creatures rose from the fires. They varied in color, but all were small and gangly with demonic horns. The creatures seemed to jump and scurry around in their individual circles, occasionally releasing a ball of fire toward Molly, but it would never penetrate her circle. Alex faded into the shadows, deciding it was better not to attract their attention.

Molly's voice became harsh and the creatures screeched in pain and grabbed their heads. They seemed to deteriorate into a red haze that left the circle and gathered in the overlapping section of the two center circles. Alex was already freaked out and a small chill spread down his spine as a large fire came to life. Flames flashed throughout the room but nothing burned.

It started at the base of the flame. Slowly, the fire organized itself into a solid substance at the bottom forming the beginnings of what looked like feet, but they seemed perfect, completely inhuman. At a sloth's pace, slender heels formed, followed by flawless, curving calf muscles and knees. Moving up, it revealed tempting thighs. Almost slowing down, it revealed well-rounded hips. Alex realized that the thing was naked and definitely female, but he couldn't look away. The gentle curve of the slender stomach was next. Slender arms unfolded from flawless breasts. The long, elegant neck gave way to a gentle chin and full lips. A cute nose and high cheekbones were created. Hauntingly seductive eyelashes opened to reveal captivating eyes. The red fire seemed to separate from the white and move up to the head to form blazing hair. The white fire became skin and the fire hair became nearly real—but too perfect to be real—constantly flowing as if alive. Alex half believed that this being had fallen from heaven, but its eyes screamed the opposite.

Her voice was clear and perfect; Alex couldn't help but stare at her utter perfection.

"What is it you seek?"

"Your soul." Molly's voice brought Alex back to reality.

The demon laughed. Still, her perfection was obvious. "My soul? Ha! Do you know who I am?"

"You are Meridiana, seducer of Gerbert."

"And poison to all men she finished. My soul has never been bound."

"I am no man and I will bind you."

"Man you are not—but that means little."

"I order you henceforth to release your soul so I may take it!"

The demon laughed, "You thought it would be that easy." Meridiana's view shifted from Molly to the corner where Alex hid. Their eyes met and Meridiana smiled seductively. Alex couldn't resist—as her charm flowed through him.

"What is it we have here?" Her eyes twinkled with seductive glee. "A man—and what a man he is." Her voice quivered with desire. "A shadow caster at that." She approached Alex, but she couldn't leave the circle. A pang of irritation and exaggerated sorrow crossed her face.

"Aw, it has been too long since I have been with a—a mortal man."

Molly must have glanced back at him, but Alex couldn't take his eyes off Meridiana long enough to notice. Molly started to chant again and Meridiana glanced at her nervously.

"Please! Oh great shadow caster, I promise you myself for all your mortal life if you ..." Meridiana glanced over angrily at Molly.

Molly was nervous now. That glance hadn't helped—she knew that she had cut off Meridiana too late. It wouldn't take much imagination to fill in the rest. Molly quickened the pace of the ritual. This was dangerous, but she wouldn't give Alex the chance to choose—or at least not enough time to come to a decision. *Why did he have to be so cocky? What an asshole.*

"So, what does he mean to you?" Molly refocused in the demon, surprised to hear her talk. She knew that she'd only cut her off from things outside the circle.

"Why?"

"The way you look at him, the way you reacted when I made my ... little offer." She sauntered around her circle, glancing seductively at Alex. Molly refused to look at him. "I could kill him, you know."

Molly almost stuttered in an important part of the ritual. *She's lying. Even if she could do anything outside the circle, which she can't, Alex is so powerful.*

The room shuddered. Darkness flowed around—enveloping all light—only to expose it at random intervals. Alex was on his knees with his arms wrapped around his head—and he was shaking uncontrollably. Turning back to Meridiana, Molly saw that her constant smile faltered as she stared at Alex.

"He's resisting." Her voice lost its confidence and her gorgeous face seemed to tremble.

"Of course he is." Ecstasy washed over Molly as she felt the ritual coming to a close. She rattled off the last parts of the spell. Meridiana's image faltered and then glowed red. Her solid form was lost as she became a red haze that joined with the faint red cloud where the circles met. It jolted from the space and slammed into Molly's chest. No impact was felt, but a sudden surge of strength radiated through her. She felt as if she was on fire, but the heat brought no pain.

Alex's stream of power ceased. The room returned to normal, and the incense ceased to burn. Alex was on his feet again—his wide eyes wouldn't leave her.

Chapter 16

Karla woke with Mike still sleeping beneath her. She stroked his hair gently as she freed herself from his muscular grasp. She was about to head over to the pile of clothes in the corner of the abandoned room when a sudden dizziness hit her and she fell on Mike.

"You okay?"

"Yeah. I'm just—I don't know. I don't feel too well, that's all."

"Oh … let me get your clothes."

Mike gathered her clothes and brought them over. He looked at her worriedly as she got dressed.

The spell passed quickly and she moved around just fine. Will and Simon arrived with James, Naomi, and Sam as soon as the smell of bacon reached their room.

Will stretched out the stiffness in his shoulders as Mike cooked. Naomi ran over and grabbed Karla's sweater.

"Sam won't stop making fun of me."

"What's Sam doing?"

"I was crying because I missed Alex and Hannah. He called me a baby and said that Alex would expect us to be strong."

Will noticed Karla's eyes flash with anger as she glared at Sam.

Sam said, "But! But … he would—he's always tough and she's supposed to be my big sis. She's supposed to be strong."

Karla's mood softened slightly, but she was still prepared to reprimand. None of this meant much to Will who—seven years older than Naomi and eight years older than Sam—had long ago blocked out their petty arguments. He was looking for the cause of Mike's concern. Karla looked perfectly healthy. In fact, she seemed to glow in spite of the laborious task of reprimanding brother and sister.

"What's wrong?" he whispered.

Mike said, "What?"

"I saw you look at Karla—you looked worried."

"Oh."

"What's wrong?" Simon asked.

"I don't know—she had a dizzy spell this morning, but she seems fine now."

"Oh." Will said.

Simon said calmly, "Mike, let me know if anything else about her changes—or if she has any more dizzy spells or any other signs of sickness."

"Okay," Mike said. "What is it?"

"Nothing. It's probably nothing."

"Simon—" Mike started as Karla approached them. She was smiling smugly, having solved another dispute.

"Hey guys."

"Hey," Simon said. "Will, are we going hunting tonight?" Hunting was the term they used to describe scavenging and stealing anything from food to money and weapons.

Will admired how smoothly Simon had transitioned their conversation.

"Uh, yeah. I guess we still need a bunch of stuff—though I hate how we're stuck here."

Karla said, "Will, you know we don't need to move and it's nice to stay put for a while. Mike! Snap out of it—I'm fine!"

"Oh, sorry."

Karla let out an exasperated sigh.

"Mike, are you coming this time? You're too stressed—it'll help." Simon patted Mike on the shoulder as he began taking the bacon off the stove.

"Yeah, sure."

"Sound more enthused—you love this stuff," Simon said, grabbing the plate Mike had just filled.

James, Naomi, and Sam claimed the next batch of bacon, while Mike and Karla ate the rest as they finished cooking. Will noticed that Karla seemed perfectly fine, healthy, and happy.

✳   ✳   ✳

Alex hovered over the woods below and let the rising sun take the chill from his shirtless body. He felt lost and confused—unable to form a coherent thought. He'd been like this since he fled her fiery grasp. He could still feel her red lips, the scent of her hair, the ecstasy of her scent, and the crimson that hovered around her deep brown eyes. She'd removed his jumpsuit and most of her clothes before he had been able to think. The only two things that passed through his mind were *Hannah* and *leave*. He'd done the latter, bursting through the apartment door in a rush of dark power that nearly ripped it off its hinges.

He felt as if he was on the verge of losing control. He trembled slightly—but not from the cold air. The winter had not yet chilled the air enough for him. He felt himself grabbing at all the power around him. He wasn't using it—just holding it. As a result, the whole forest was still—nothing was able to move against his will.

❋　❋　❋

Molly held her knees against her breasts in the cold water. Glancing into the mirror, she gazed at her slightly altered appearance. Her eyes had taken on a reddish hue that startled her. Her hair also had far more red in it. Her body had changed as well; the curves of her body had been enhanced and her clothes fit differently—tighter in some places and looser in others. None of this bothered her. All she could think of was Alex. He'd come to her so willingly and then suddenly he was gone. She hated him for it, but mostly she hated not understanding him and not having him.

Growing uncomfortable, she allowed the water to drain from the tub. She stepped toward the mirror and she stared at her unfamiliar red-brown eyes. Searching inside herself, she found the power that now resided there. Its heat increased her body temperature by at least five degrees, making her hot to the touch. She had noticed this the night before when Alex touched her and he felt surprisingly cold.

Reaching for the power, she increased the amount of heat released into her. Her body began to steam as the water evaporated. She kept enjoying the warmth that nearly exceeded the fire still burning from the night before. Suddenly, her hand was on fire. Surprised, she jumped back. Losing focus, her temperature returned to what it had been before and the fire went out in her hand.

Cursing silently, she grabbed a bathrobe and left the bathroom. Lying on the bed, she opened up Lasorian's book. She hit herself mentally because she'd forgotten that imps conjured fire that they hurled at their enemies. One of the reasons she chose imps was to strengthen herself—as well as her ritual—before summoning Meridiana. Having bound six to herself, she'd be able to create a pretty substantial attack without much effort. Lifting up her hand and focusing on it, she willed her powers to heat it. Prepared this time, she was only slightly startled when her hand burst into flame.

Trying not to lose focus, she tried to shape the flame. Slowly, it condensed until it sat in the palm of her hand, instead of encompassing the entire thing. She tried to move it away from her hand, but she failed and the fire went out. Trying again, she called the fire into her palm and sent it out in front of her. She moved the hovering fireball about five feet in front and tried to move it with speed back and forth. This wasn't very difficult.

Feeling confident, she let the fire go out. Now focusing on the lampshade of one of the lamps Alex had destroyed, she tried to will it on fire. Nothing happened and she tried until she was sure it was futile. *I guess I can only bring fire out of my body—I can't call it elsewhere.* Flipping through the book again, she came to the part on magic words. She'd studied this part earlier, but not nearly as thoroughly as the rituals. She quickly compiled a makeshift spell. Facing the lampshade again, she uttered the spell and it burst into flame. Surprised at how violently it burned, she ran over and quickly smothered it. She cursed herself for not having made a spell to put out the fire. Falling back on the bed, she stared at the remnants of the lampshade before continuing to study the book.

❋　❋　❋

Alex felt his anger ebb. No longer risking losing control, he let warmth flow through him to melt the cold that kept him sane. Now able to think, he released his grip on the world around him.

Beneath him, things erupted in motion, animals kept strained by his grip now ran or flew around violently in fear and confusion. The treetops stirred with whatever birds had not moved on for the winter as they fled the area in fear of whatever had held them, trapped, inside their own bodies.

He tried to take his mind off of the night before. A crow flying beneath him served as a distraction. It flew in confused circles, gaining height slowly until he was able to get a better look at it. It was very large for a crow; he noticed he had misjudged its size as it flew closer and closer in tighter circles.

"Are you going to hover there all day or are you going to prepare to stop Zanier?" Alex recognized Lasorian's voice.

"You can change form too?"

"Only into a raven. It's a perk of one of the demons I have bound to myself."

"How many demons have you bound?" Alex watched the crow change back into his human shape.

"Not looking too good. You tried sleeping lately?"

Alex stared back at Lasorian coldly.

"I assume Molly's ritual went well. I can still feel that succubus' spell around you. You shattered it maybe, but the smell of it … so alluring. Oh how confused must Molly be? You must have come to her at first? How quickly did you leave? How hurt is she?"

Alex turned away, though none of the ice left his eyes. "It doesn't matter."

"Really? I thought she was a tad bit more than a tool to you. I guess I overestimated your compassion."

"She is not a tool."

Lasorian seemed pleased at Alex's reaction. "But she will no doubt help against Zanier."

Alex glared at Lasorian. "I never asked her to—and I won't let her."

"Really? I thought she didn't matter to you? And who are you to say what she can and cannot do?"

"Who are you to tell me what I can and cannot do? It was you who said I was the most powerful being on this world." Alex's voice hadn't lost any of its cold edge, but it held a newfound fury.

"Most dangerous—not most powerful. Not yet—there is quite a difference."

"What does it matter—it's close enough."

"Don't push me, Alex. Look around you. This is not your domain. Don't underestimate me."

"What can you do? I can kill you where you stand without any effort—nothing can block my powers." He was bluffing; he couldn't recall exactly what the darkness made him do.

"Fool! You think I will fail like some half-rate mage? I wouldn't dare approach you this way unless I was sure I was more powerful. I even bet you have no idea what it was you did that night"

Alex didn't respond, nor did he stop gathering power. Once again, they locked eyes. Alex saw his confidence and wavered.

"Good—now stop acting like a fool and do something. Get ready! You can't go into a fight in your underwear—no matter how powerful you are. No victory is worth winning while the opponent and the entire crowd laugh at you."

"Where did you hear that? Some old gladiator comic book?"

"No. I believe I heard it from a gladiator himself."

Alex watched Lasorian pass through an arch of flame that wrapped around him. *He's right—I need to prepare.* Grabbing the power around him, he vanished into shadow.

He felt the ground of the apartment, half amazed that he'd been able to teleport with such precision. Molly was at the foot of the bed and had pulled her bathrobe tightly around herself.

Alex had to turn away—it was all he could do not to look into her eyes or follow the curve of her legs that the bathrobe didn't hide.

"You're back." Alex listened to her statement, but couldn't respond. As calmly as he could, he gathered his gear. "So you're not going to talk—can't you stand to look at me?"

Alex looked at her for a second, but cursed himself for it. He saw the sorrow that she was trying to hide. "What do you want?" He felt himself go cold—he hated himself for being so empty to her.

She struggled to say something as he donned his bulletproof suit. Putting on his cape, he turned so his back was completely to her.

Alex stepped back in surprise when a wall of fire rose in front of him. He saw Molly walking at him furiously. "You think you can ignore me? I don't care what the hell your feelings are for that other girl—I know you like me. You're not as impenetrable as you may think. Look at me, Alex." She was closer now and Alex didn't obey. A sharp burst of pain scorched his left cheek. He felt his face and realized that she'd slapped him. Her hand was on fire, but he remained silent.

Alex began to gather power to teleport when Molly's voice broke his concentration. "You're not leaving, Alex! I know that Zanier won't attack Savannah till night and it's not even noon. You have time."

"To what? Talk? I don't particularly feel like that right now."

"What happened last night? Why did you leave? Alex, answer me!"

The fire behind Alex reared as it matched her emotion. Her hands caught fire, but did not burn her skin. The bathrobe was another story as it slowly began to singe.

In frustration, Alex lashed out in a burst of power. The wall of flame vanished. As Molly braced herself and lost concentration, all her spells were interrupted. She fell to her knees, grasping at her head from a sudden headache.

He realized she was crying. Several seconds passed and she didn't move from that position. Alex couldn't decide between comforting her and ending it forever.

Not knowing when he made the choice, he knelt down beside her. Brushing the hair from her face, he looked into her eyes. He wiped the tears away and rested his hand on her neck.

"Sorry."

"Leave."

Alex was surprised by the cold in her sobbing voice, but he didn't argue. He was about to stand when he felt Molly's hand brush his. "I'll be there—don't try to stop me." Alex nodded, focused, and vanished.

Molly found herself staring at the spot were Alex had been. That he had gotten angry enough to lash out with magic truly hurt her.

She hated him for apologizing and hated him for trying to comfort her. She hated him for giving her pathetic soul hope. If he had just left her on the ground, she could have loathed him for being so cold. She began throwing clothes on the ground, covering the circles on the ground. She realized how pathetically suited any of them would be for fighting.

Chapter 17

The water shifted in color with the fading light in front of Alex. How long ago was it that he could have watched this without half the cares he had now? It felt like years. A sound of crunching sand caught Alex's attention. A figure in a green robe walked calmly across the beach below him. He had watched Zanier's mercenaries swing away from Savannah out toward Tybee Island. They had several mages accompanying them. He had recognized Hannah with them and had to follow them.

Hannah had separated from them, now she walked the beach alone. Alex had flown ahead of her and waited for her to make her way up the beach. She recognized him and ran up the beach.

"Hannah!"

"Alex!" She hugged him. At first, Alex couldn't breathe, but her grip loosened and Alex returned the embrace. Her body felt wonderful in his arms. He had missed her excited breathing and the smell of her light brown hair.

"Alex, you're back. What's wrong?"

"I'm not back."

"What do you mean—you're here?"

"I'm here to fight Zanier. I'm *here* to see you."

"Alex ..."

"Please, Hannah. Listen to me."

"Alex, please don't."

"Hannah, Zanier is conquering America for his own means. You don't actually believe he's going to give up any power."

"No, I don't, but I have seen him already start to stabilize places we've been. He's using magic to help people."

"And what about those who can't?"

"They'll still have jobs and better lives. There won't be any more of the chaos that we went through."

"Hannah, I'm sure he's giving them all this, but think about it, he's going to take away their rights. He's just going to be another dictator."

"Alex, please don't make me choose."

"Choose what?"

"Between you or Zanier's cause."

"Hannah, I can't let him do this."

"Then come back to us. If you're as strong as they say now, compete with him. Make him listen so that when we do reshape this world, your point of view can be seen."

"Hannah, I don't want that."

"What? So you're willing to sit back and comment on other people's ideas to fix the world, but you only get in their way because you think they're wrong—and you do nothing!" She suddenly drew closer to him. "Alex, I know you—and that's not you. Don't give me crap about not being leader material—you led us out of trouble and brought us here."

Alex asked, "How are the others doing?"

"I don't know. I haven't been back to the boat for a while."

"Check up on them for me."

Hannah took a step back and crossed her arms. "Why don't you? Seeing that you're coming with me, don't try to change the subject"

"Hannah—"

"Alex, what are you going to do—stop him? He has over a hundred mages now and even more being trained. Are you going to try to stop everyone! Why don't you go stop the invasion in China or the civil war in the Middle East! As well as stopping the one here! Alex, you're one person. You can't change the world by yourself!"

"I can try—and I can't let Zanier do this!"

"Alex, I understand that Zanier isn't perfect, but he's giving people hope when it's been so long since anyone has had any. He won't make the world perfect, but perhaps he can bring stability to at least part of the world so that positive change can happen."

"Hannah, I'm sorry."

Her hand cupped the side of his face and drew it toward her own. Her lips touched his—he was kissing her before he even realized it. No regrets passed through him as he gave himself to her. He wanted her more and more as his hands moved along her back and into her hair.

Alex soon felt himself trip and dragged Hannah with him onto the sand. The fall had forced them to separate and their argument had been forgotten. Alex watched her beautiful green eyes as she undid his cape.

Reaching down to her ankles and feeling the curves of her long legs, he lifted her robe. She raised her arms and let it fall off. She laughed when he rolled so she was under him. She wasn't wearing much under the robe—just fleece pants and a tight pajama top. As he bent down to kiss her again, he took in her body. It was much the same as he remembered—except she no longer looked starved without an ounce flesh on her bones. Her full breasts attracted him as he thought of kissing them. Releasing her grip, she started taking off his suit. Alex went to kiss her again, but she agilely moved out from under him. She removed her clothes and ran to the water. He finished taking off his bulletproof suit and ran after her. The water wasn't bad for being so close to winter, but Alex was forced to force the cold away as he swam after her. She waited for him and giggled when he grabbed her waist.

Alex found it awkward to swim and make out with her at the same time. He gave up and floated on his back. They stared at the sky and held hands.

"Alex?"

"Yes."

"Please don't go."

"Hannah, I have to."

"I know. Please just be careful."

He swam closer to her and kissed her. They watched the sunset and, without saying a word, swam back to shore.

CHAPTER 18

The twilight grew fainter and a faint breeze ruffled Zanier's green robes. He watched Hannah's approach from the open area of suburbs surrounding the city. The sun was almost set and no resistance had yet been met. Alex had appeared moments ago levitating above the main part of the city by the river.

"Are we to attack?" Kyle asked.

"Wait for Hannah."

Zanier watched Kyle turn toward her. She didn't seem to be in too much of a rush. Walking slowly, her eyes turned to where Alex floated.

"She won't fight him."

"No, but she'll fight whatever other resistance we face. Alex won't be too much of a problem. There are far too many of us."

"Her hair is wet," Kyle said. "She went swimming."

Zanier asked, "Hannah, what took you?"

"Nothing—I just wanted to walk on the beach."

Zanier didn't bother looking at her; he could hear the lie in her voice.

"We will talk later. Kyle, start the attack."

※　※　※

Alex watched the mass of mages and soldiers move. He watched Molly walk down the street. A pang of guilt ran through him, but he quickly turned away. He had done what he had to and couldn't be distracted now.

He felt the power he'd been collecting around him shift with anticipation of what was to come. A wall of darkness fifty stories high rose and stretched the entire width of the city and arched to touch each bank of the river behind him. Anyone who tried to pass through it would have his or her energy sapped. The body would shut down before it reached the other side.

The approaching army halted in awe of what they saw. Confusion flew through the ranks of the mages and the soldiers. A smaller group of mages took to the air and approached him. There were about forty in total and apparently the only ones with power enough to spare for combat and flight.

Alex wrestled with the darkness he was using for the wall. He tied it off so that it would draw its own power through the shadows, using him as the link through which the power would flow so he wouldn't have to focus on it. If he wasn't forced to handle so much power at once, it would be easier on him mentally and he would have to worry less about losing control. This was the largest amount of power he had ever tied off and the mages were approaching quickly. He finally finished tying off the wall of darkness

"Alex! Leave now or come back with us. You cannot stand against us."

Zanier floated several feet higher about ten yards away. "I think I can take the forty of you," Alex said. He was glad not to see Hannah in that forty—he didn't want to think what would happen if he was forced to fight her as well.

Walking the streets of Savannah, Hannah was surprised to not see anyone else. There was no resistance—not a living thing. Zanier had told her to search for any resistance and—short of Alex—she couldn't find anything. Hannah felt shivers as she looked back at the wall of darkness. It felt of death merely coming within fifty feet of it—she didn't dare think of what would happen if she tried to go through it.

The city's buildings were sealed up tight or vacated. She figured that most had evacuated to some sort of safe house or locked themselves in the basements. She prayed that Alex was going to be okay as she saw Zanier and about forty mages approach him.

"Impressive, isn't he?"

"Who are you?" she asked.

The girl in front of her was probably two years older than she was. She had long auburn hair and she was very pretty. She was wearing jeans and a flowing white top.

"I'm Molly. Why aren't you up there with all the other mages?"

"I wouldn't dare harm him!" Hannah raised a hand to her mouth, surprised at her outburst.

"You're Hannah, aren't you? You're pretty. I'll give you that—though for such a young girl, he seems to remember you at the worst possible times. How old are you? Fourteen? Fifteen?"

"Sixteen! What do you have to do with Alex? What do you mean he remembers me at the worst possible times?" *Why was she talking about Alex this way? Why did she keep looking at him that way?*

"Well, we had the date the first day we spent in the apartment. He was a little shy about sharing a bed."

"You slept in the same bed? You went on a date? Who are you?"

"He's a very good kisser too. There was that time after he went after those two mages—and last night, he had the awful timing to remember you both times. The last time was right when I had nearly finished taking all his clothes off."

"You were ... he was ... but he?" Hannah couldn't form a coherent thought. She had not realized that her feelings for Alex were so strong till the beach. *Yes, he is a very good kisser!*

"You're the girl on the news."

Hannah was surprised at the moisture in her eyes.

"Yup, I guess everyone saw that."

"Leave Alex alone! He's mine! I love him!"

Molly said, "I have to say the same to you because I love him as well. I never thought a boy could make me into an idiot."

Hannah wasn't sure who had started it, but pale gold lightning streaked from her hands and fireballs shot from Molly's hands.

✳   ✳   ✳

Alex deftly avoided a fireball and the dark blue lightning. The first few moments of the battle had been a revelation to Alex. He hadn't realized how weak these mages were—compared to him—or how long it took them to straighten out their attacks. *I guess aerial group combat against one person wasn't part of the training.* Except for Zanier, Kyle, and Tantalus, very few posed any reasonable threat. Three-fourths of the group was guardians leaving ten points in which he could receive any real harm and from that ten maybe four had a chance of breaking through his shield if they caught him off guard. That just left a very annoying shield held by thirty mages that surrounded all of them. He had yet to get through it. He knew he could completely avoid it but memories from that night when he'd killed Charles were hazy and he only had a vague idea of what he had done.

With a quick burst of power, he sped under and behind the main group. A massive ball of shadow energy flew from his hands and struck into the invisible shield. He had been conserving power for a while so that he could unleash so much power. The shield shook, but held. In a few moments, Kyle and Tantalus would be on him—they had always been the quickest. He shot a quick spear of power at the mass of guardians, aiming for a single mage. When it struck the shield, it broke through and pierced it. The remnant that broke through struck the guardian squarely in the head. He appeared shocked as his eyes rolled back and he fell. Alex was sure that the attack had only knocked him out, but the fall would kill him.

Alex quickly refocused on defending himself. Kyle was on him and, an instant later, Tantalus was as well. Fire and lightning streaked toward him. He didn't dodge them—he took them with his shields and sent bursts at them. They avoided them and kept up their own power. Alex dodged, focusing on the stationary mound of guardians. Soon he'd have too many war mages on him to attack. He launched several barrages of shadow energy at the group. Not used to evasive flying, most struck home, punching through the shield and mages dropped like flies.

Panic streaked across Zanier's face, but he had avoided all of Alex's attacks. The attacks ceased as the remaining mages tried to halt their comrades from plummeting to earth.

Alex had won and ceased his assault. Two people dueling with magic grabbed his attention about a quarter mile away.

Alex remembered that Molly had been in the city. Fear struck him with surprising strength as he teleported.

His vision blurred. The wall didn't react well to his teleportation. A surge of power rushed through him and he struggled to stand. Two attacks hit him on either side, his shield struggled to stand. Standing up and clutching his stomach, he saw Molly and Hannah staring at him. Their faces could have been mirrors. Anger shifted to concern and back to anger as they saw that he was unharmed.

"What's going on?" He meant to be firm, but he choked out the words.

"Alex, let's go," Molly said, striding toward him a hint more seductively than she ever had before.

"This woman—or whatever she is—tells me that you nearly had sex with her before you conveniently remembered that I existed."

"You were hardly together—so shut up, girl! You merely had a crush on him. However, we've had a bit more than that—haven't we, Alex? You run off and make out with this thing on the beach!"

"I told you—"

"You were lying through your teeth—you couldn't even look!"

"What? Did he tell you he didn't have feelings for you?"

"Hannah, I'm sorry for what I did," Molly's hand left the side of his face numb and hot.

Molly strutted through an arch of flame with a hazy light inside. The sound of her crying burned into his ears as the arch closed.

"You do have feelings for her. What I'd give to have you look at me that way."

"Hannah, I—"

"Alex, you need to straighten out whatever is happening inside your head. You can't love two people—it'll only hurt them." Alex cupped the side of Hannah's face, brushing away her hair and tears.

"Hannah, I love you." She flung her hands around and kissed him. Alex never wanted to let her go, but eventually she pushed away.

"Good-bye, Alex. Come see me again if you straighten out your feelings."

She left without looking back, leaving Alex alone in the street. He realized that his breathing was heavy and it wasn't from exertion or stress. He was furious—angry with Zanier for changing everything, angry at Lasorian for teaching Molly how to bind, angry at Molly for ruining his relationship with Hannah, angry at Hannah for not choosing him over Zanier's cause, and angry with himself for being too weak and getting himself into this situation.

Alex hadn't realized that he'd been calling power to himself the entire time. He laughed at the coldness inside of him. He was death—and any who approached him now would meet death.

✳   ✳   ✳

Molly's tears turned to steam and she struggled to take a solid breath in her travels. The demonic doorway was not as quick as Alex's way of teleporting, but it allowed her to travel long distances in a small period of time. From Savannah to the apartment would take her about twenty minutes. It was time to straighten herself out. *He'll be there when I get back—once he's done with that bitch.* She couldn't decide whether she wanted him to be there or not. She hated him and would not mind hitting him a few more times.

She traveled through a portal that looked like an arched hallway wrought from fire—except for a small patch on the floor. She crossed her arms as if she was cold—despite the heat and the sweat that rolled down her face as she thought about returning to the apartment. He would have to be back by the time she got back. His means of travel was instant and didn't risk burning anything. She had to walk from the woods to the apartment. He would have to come back. *Of course he'd come back. Where else would he go—to Zanier with that girl? He wouldn't. What if he didn't come back? It's not like he has to sleep. I wish he would sleep. He looks so tired. I don't care what he says. Screw him—why should I care? He can get as tired looking as he wants for all I care. I hope he chokes while kissing that bitch! No, I don't. Damn him! He'll be there before I get back. I have to calm down.*

The portal came to an end surprisingly quickly and spit her out into the woods. Turning, she carefully suppressed a small fire on the grass. Taking a deep breath, she slowly started through the woods to the apartment.

Before the past month, she might have been nervous walking through the woods in the pitch dark. Now she felt nothing—only concentrating on how she was going to deal with confronting Alex. Clearing the edge of the woods, she was debating hitting him or kissing him and trying the thing that Lasorian had mentioned that would halt Alex from trying to teleport—unless he tried very hard. She was confident enough that she could make him not want to try very hard. She might have blushed at the idea of that once—not so long ago—but she cared little about that when she reached the top of the stairs.

She knocked on the door, but no one answered. *All right, be like that.* She was leaning toward hitting him again. Hoping he would open it, she spent much longer than she had to open the door. The apartment was dark. *He better not be sulking.* She flicked on the lights. She looked around, but he wasn't there at all.

She felt cold as she sat down on the bed—something that didn't seem natural. Since she bound the demons, she had always felt warm. She undressed and crawled into the bed. *He'll be here soon. I better not fall asleep or he'll get off too easily.* Losing her battle against weariness, she drifted to sleep.

Hannah stared back at the wall of darkness that she had just flown over. *What I did was for the best. He's confused and needs time to straighten things out. He'll come to me. I need to stop worrying about it.* She walked back to the camp that Zanier had begun setting up. She understood that Alex needed time to realize that Zanier and the mages were not the enemy. They could stop the chaos in America and help stop what had happened to them and all their friends from happening to others.

She pulled her cloak tighter as she entered the camp. It was quite cold and she didn't like wasting power to warm herself.

"Hannah!"

She turned as a plump girl ran up to her.

"Sara told me to get you. She needs anyone with any ability in healing to come take care of those who were injured fighting Alex. No one's died so far, but there are some severe injuries."

Hannah could have chosen to be a healer or a war mage. It was rare, but the talent left her a little weaker than someone of her own ability that had only pure talent in one. Sara was a purely talented healer, but not near Hannah's strength. Hannah could never hope to compete with her in healing. Where Kyle was much the same way with war magic, she had decided to focus in war magic because she wanted to fight to change the world. Kyle told her that she wouldn't develop as quickly as most close to her strength due to her double talent, but she discovered that few of the other mages were near her level of strength. Even Kyle admitted that she would one day be greater than him—and he was second to only Zanier. He admitted not knowing exactly how strong Zanier was—just that he had done things with war magic as a guardian that Kyle could hardly believe. He wasn't sure whether Zanier was double talented, but thought that he might be. Otherwise no one could touch him—except maybe Alex. Alex had proven tonight that he wasn't to be taken lightly.

"I'm coming—lead the way." The girl nodded and took off back toward the camp.

"Sara said something about their minds being affected by his attacks. They keep mumbling about being cold when their body temperatures were normal. Sara couldn't figure it out with her probing—and didn't want to waste time—so she pumped them full of healing magic. It did the trick, but it required a lot of power and—since most of the mages that went up there were hit—they were running low on healers that haven't exhausted themselves yet."

"Hannah, this way."

Sara dragged her through a mass of cots with men and women on them. She counted thirty-two—only eight had avoided the attack. "Here—get to pumping these five full of power. When you're done, let me know how you're feeling. There are ten more after these." Sara's beautiful face was marred by dark circles under her eyes. *How far had she exhausted herself?*

Without a moment of hesitation, she started healing. What she was going to do was fairly simple—she just needed skin contact. The girl had been right—the man she had just grabbed was shivering despite his normal temperature. Flooding his body with healing magic, he shuddered and stopped shivering. Quickly she moved between the other four, but weariness began to set in. The battle with the girl had taken a lot out of her. *I can't believe he let her touch him.* Sara gestured to another group on the cots. Finishing another three, she saw that seven had been taken care of.

Kyle had made it to the healing compound and was helping Sara walk by supporting her with an arm around her waist and an arm around his shoulder. She could tell that they loved each other. *It would be nice if Alex was here to help support me. I may not need it, but I want it!* She walked over to where Kyle had found chairs for them.

"Sara, let me get rid of some of your weariness."

"I'm fine, Hannah. You must be tired."

"Sara, she's not tired yet and you should look at yourself— you look awful," he said, frowning at her. "I mean you look really tired—let her heal you."

Not waiting for a response, she touched Sara's wrist and began to heal. The basic routine was to search through a person's body with magic to check if there was anything else wrong with them. It was the first thing they taught in healing—even war mages with no other ability knew how to do it—even if that was all they could do. Sara's body felt healthy, but off in some way—from the arm to the chest to the head to her other arm and down into her abdomen. When she got to the uterus she stopped—it took a moment to realize what she was feeling. Sara noticed that she had stopped and was suddenly trying to force her out of her body. Quickly Hannah cleansed Sara's weariness and pulled out.

When her sight returned, Sara was staring at her.

"Don't say anything."

The patches under her eyes were gone—the eyes were pure intensity. If she had meant for Kyle not to hear those words, she had failed.

Kyle gripped Hannah's wrist. "What's wrong with her? I felt her try to force you out and fail. You found something! What is it?"

"There's nothing wrong with me, Kyle!" Sara said, firmly placing a hand on Kyle's elbow.

"Then why try to force her out?"

"She's pregnant!" Hannah blurted out.

Sara closed her eyes as she sunk back into her chair. Kyle's eyes softened as he held Sara's hand. Hannah swore that she had never seen so many emotions flash across a man's face. He also looked as though he couldn't decide whether to sit or stand. Hannah decided to leave them alone.

Sara gently put a hand on his, but he didn't seem to feel it.

"Sara, why didn't you want to tell me? I'll be a good father and I know you may not want to marry me yet, but I love—" Sara's fingers tightened around Kyle's hand.

"Stop! Of course I love you—and yes I want to marry you!"

She tried to stand, but began to drop back down in exhaustion. Kyle caught her and helped her to her feet.

"Kyle, I didn't want to tell you—or anybody—because I was afraid of your reaction. Not just yours, but Zanier's and the rest of the mages. I don't want to be kept from the front lines. I'm the strongest healer. I have to be there. I don't want to be treated like a breakable doll!"

Kyle pulled her closer and she collapsed into his chest. She hadn't realized that she was trembling until Kyle began trying to comfort her. "Don't worry. I don't think Zanier would take you away from healing the mages, but don't think for a second that I won't be watching you and keeping you from trying to do more than you can."

"Of course not," she said. As she felt herself start to collapse, Kyle lifted her up.

※　※　※

Alex shuddered as the power surged through him. His stomach felt like emptying itself. He realized that he was losing control and was holding enough power to level the city in a heartbeat. The wall was forcing him to pull in more. Alex was trying to untie the flow of power to the wall when he felt the knot. It had become solid and it was impossible for him to undo it. Grabbing at his own supply of power, he tried to sever the flow and was met with immense resistance. Almost as a reaction to his attack, power surged through him again. This time he fell to his knees and began dry heaving.

Hearing footsteps next to him, he looked up to see Lasorian. Lasorian kneeled beside Alex and lifted him to his feet. Alex's body was weak and trembling. "Fight it, boy! Unless you want to die and perhaps take a few with you for your fool mistake, teleporting like you did forced the tide of power to reform on its own—crude yet solid. Now you fight against more power than you can safely control!"

"I . . . am!" Alex struggled to stay on his feet. The power surged again and the nausea hit. His sight blurring, Alex lost balance and fell. Darkness crept closer around the edge of his vision. Fighting for control, Alex never felt Lasorian catch him. All he could do was struggle against the cold and emotionless darkness that sought to control him.

✳ ✳ ✳

Hannah watched the wall of darkness from the safety of the mages' camp. It had been a while since she had left Kyle and Sara. The wall shuddered—Hannah was sure of it. *What are you doing, Alex?* It shuddered violently again and clouds of darkness flew off like dust in a wind. Hannah took a step back when it shuddered again. The ground moaned as the wall grew half again as tall as it had been.

Zanier was staring at the wall and Tantalus was at his left shoulder.

"What is Alex doing? We ended our attack," Tantalus said.

"I think he might be in some kind of difficulty—this may be like when he killed Charles," Zanier said. "Perhaps we pushed him too far. It was unbelievable that he was able to handle so many of us like we were nothing—but maybe he was at his limit."

"What do you mean?" Hannah yelled.

"Where he loses control of the power. You know how the darkness can control him. I've been doing a lot more research into it since that day. Alex is in a constant battle of wills against the darkness. The more power he seeks to control, the harder he needs to concentrate."

"What happens if he loses control?"

"The darkness will take control of him. Judging from what's going on, I'd say he hasn't lost full control yet. Perhaps he can hold on, but either way I'm readying the mages. We're going to have to put up a barrier between us and the city."

Hannah was about to lift herself into the air when she felt something solid separate herself from her power. She gasped at the loss of joy and the rush of her power suddenly being taken away.

"Don't be foolish, girl. There is nothing you can do for him. Even if he wins this struggle tonight, he has been influenced by darkness. Alex has been gone since he began controlling more darkness than his store. The magic he uses is evil!"

Hannah blinked and was surprised at the moistness in her eyes. "What did you do?"

"I blocked you. I will unblock you when you come back into camp with me." Hannah tried to reach her power again. Zanier was using an unbelievable amount of power to keep her from reaching her own. He had created what felt like a shell around it. She turned to follow Zanier. *Alex, please be okay.*

✻   ✻   ✻

Molly awoke to a knock on her door. *What took him so long?* It had been nearly two hours since she had left Alex in Savannah.

Before she opened the door, she knew it wasn't Alex. She could feel the demonic flows of power that came off a warlock casting or maintaining a spell.

Lasorian stood outside her door, his bizarrely colored eyes visible in the darkness.

"You are needed—or else Alex may die."

"What?" Molly felt cold fear in her chest "What happened to him?"

"He teleported while maintaining a flow of darkness. It's drawing more power through him than he can control. He

needs some motivation to fight it and you're giving it to him."
Molly stepped out of the door to see what Lasorian was
maintaining. A familiar arch of fire formed on the cement
walkway.

"I'll try, but he made it pretty clear—" Her breath caught
as she looked through the arch. The image was clear. Alex
was unconscious on pavement. Without a thought, she ran
through the portal, stumbling slightly. As she passed through
the archway, she fell onto Alex.

He was ice cold. The only sign of life was his eyes. His
lips were blue and his skin was white.

"Molly?" Alex whimpered.

"Yes, Alex. I'm here."

"No!" Alex screamed. "Why?" His eyes searched till he
found Lasorian behind her. "You brought her here! Why?
Leave now!"

"No!"

Alex screamed as if pierced by a thousand burning stakes.
His body arched in spasm. Darkness flowed out of his eyes
and mouth. Molly struggled to hold him down.

To Molly's shock, Alex laughed madly. "Not only do I
die here, but I kill her too! My shade will haunt you for the
rest of your days for this, Lasorian! I am going to die! And
now you are making me kill her!"

Lasorian stared coldly at Alex.

"Alex! I'm here on my own—I won't let you die!" Molly
screamed.

"Molly?"

She threw herself on him and kissed him. The darkness
coming from his mouth was colder than his lips, but she didn't
care. She needed him to fight so that he would return to her.
To her surprise, he kissed back for a moment. Suddenly, she

felt herself being thrown off by an invisible force. Lasorian's hand caught her arm and steadied her.

Alex's body arched once more before he floated into the air and settled on his feet. A thoughtful expression on his face, he stretched a hand out to his side and flexed his fingers. Molly suddenly felt relieved. *He's okay!* Taking a step forward, she felt Lasorian throw her behind him.

"So this is what happens when the darkness takes you," Lasorian stated coolly.

"Lasorian? Ah, that is what this boy's memory names you. Hmm. It seems several of us remember you by that name as well." Alex's voice sounded like many different men's voices overlapping each other. "No, this is not what happens when the darkness takes you. We took him from it—what a waste if he died or was slaughtered before he got a chance to truly master what he is—like so many of us." The voices laughed many different laughs. "No, we took him from the darkness. When we release him, he'll be fine—he may even remember some of this." Alex cracked his neck.

"Was that you, Remus—or perhaps Romulus? You were both so similar in your mannerisms." It sounded as if only two voices laughed. "It seems you all remember me in some way. It seems my theories about the death of the shadow caster were not too far off."

"A shadow caster doesn't die—he is merely reclaimed by the shadows from where he came. Enough of this. We've always wanted to see what our combined skills could do. Lasorian, what do you say? You are no pushover. From what I can feel, you are even stronger. How about it? This boy did seem to get himself in quite the mess. Good thing that several of us have some experience with this type of thing—right, brother?" Molly felt a burst of air behind her, but didn't turn to see the wall dissipate into the air.

"Lasorian, ready yourself. We fight."

Molly stared in awe at Alex as all the voices spewed out of him—each belonging to a different person.

"Poe, Mathieu, Remus, Romulus, Jacob, Howe, Hiro, Mercian, Ryan, Marcus, Cyrus—let's fight." Alex's smile— still distorted by the darkness spewing from his mouth—was quite clear. He stretched his hands out and lights, shapes, and images seemed to bend as Alex pulled the darkness toward him.

A barrier of light was thrown up around Alex and he seemed to dissipate from it. Lasorian suddenly shot into the air, hurling golden fireballs into the sky. Molly quickly called the power she needed to fly and lifted herself onto the tallest building she could see.

She caught sight of Alex several yards behind Lasorian. Lightning bloomed from the dark mist that surrounded Alex's hands, slammed into Lasorian's shield, and crackled as if angry at being halted. When Lasorian turned, Alex was gone—but the sky was suddenly alive. Lightning hooked and arched across the sky—Lasorian couldn't do anything except try to avoid them and block the bolts with his shields.

The amount of power that Lasorian wielded was unreal. He must not have been joking when he talked about the amount of demons that he'd bound to himself. One of the lightning bolts would have penetrated any protection she could use against it—judging by the surges in Lasorian's shields whenever they hit it.

Molly couldn't find Alex anywhere that the lightning was streaming from—despite the randomness and the number of spots that it was coming from. Molly began to notice a pattern in the lightning, that it was coming from the same places Molly spotted Alex floating a few hundred yards away from the battle.

Molly watched him in fear and amazement. Light from the side caught her attention—a massive fireball was heading toward her. Before she could raise a shield, Alex was in front of her. The ball of golden flame collided against a barrier of darkness.

"He seems to love you. It's so strange to be in love with two women. Oh, the pain that will be done to his heart."

Molly's heart pounded and voices rang in her head. *He loves me? He loves two women!*

Alex saw Lasorian not ten feet away and Alex's hands were suddenly hazed in darkness. Molly could see sparks inside the darkness that surrounded his hands. Lasorian was gone, but lightning headed straight toward them.

Alex charged at them and seemed to be consumed by the lightning as it arched around him. The bolts that streaked toward him swirled around him, illuminating him in a pale blue light. As suddenly as they had surrounded him, they streaked down his outstretched hand toward Lasorian. Lightning struck his shield and shattered it. Instead of scorching him, they wrapped tightly around him. Molly watched Lasorian stiffen as he floated toward Alex.

"It seems several of us have soft hearts—but unlike you, we're not willing to risk her to win. Ha—not a bad tactic if we must say. I should have realized you'd be more powerful together than any of you ever were apart."

"That would have been wise," Alex said. "It was nice to flex our wills after so long just feeling darkness, but all things come to an end. So long, Lasorian—it was nice to duel you again."

"Same to you—perhaps it would be wise to leave the lightning secret with Alex."

"Perhaps—but I believe it will be better to let him figure that out on his own." The darkness flowing from his eyes and mouth began to slow, "Good-bye, Lasorian, Molly." Alex's body went limp as the darkness flowing from his eyes and mouth faded. Molly ran to catch him; he fell unconscious into her arms, forcing her to her knees.

Molly felt Alex's breath on her neck and his head on her shoulder. She brushed her hand through his hair and realized it was black. That surprised her for she remembered it being dark brown. Lasorian put a hand on her shoulder and she felt him weaving demonic powers into a spell. She tried to watch, but whatever he was doing was beyond her. An arch of fire wrapped around them. Lasorian took his hand from her shoulder. Molly looked around the inside of the apartment. She saw Lasorian walk through an archway of fire that opened in front of him. Molly expected to see fire damage on the floor, but saw nothing.

Alex stirred in her arms. "Shh … I'll help you into bed."

"I can't."

Molly was surprised to hear him speak—even if he sounded incoherent. Struggling to lift him, Molly got him onto the bed. Alex opened his eyes when his head hit the pillow. Molly gasped and stepped back. They were ice blue. "Alex, your eyes …"

He sighed and his head fell back on the pillow. "I can feel you. I can feel your fear. I can feel your worry. I'm not even trying. Ha—I felt them in my head. I don't know what they did—everything is more focused. There's a dog in the floor below us that is feeling joy over his new bone. There's a middle-aged couple cuddling three rooms away that just had the greatest sex they've had in long time. On the first floor, a drunken man is alone and contemplating his life. A girl fears for her life in the darkness. Her mother is in pain and her father is—"

"Stop it, Alex! Stop!"

"All that touches shadow I can feel."

"Alex!" Molly crawled next to him and stared into his cruel blue eyes. "Go to sleep—you went through a lot today. Please go to sleep."

Alex laughed quietly. Molly would not have heard it if she had not been so close. Together they drifted into unsettled dreams.

Zanier stared at the empty sky above Savannah. The light show had startled everyone in the camp. He and Tantalus were the only ones that could feel any of it. He had a different reason to stare at the sky. He had learned how to perform a difficult spell that allowed him to sense demonic magic. Tantalus seemed to be able to do so on his own. He had sensed ample amounts—enough to question his own strength against the warlock. He figured it was Lasorian, but he had defeated him those years ago. It was always possible that he had bound more demons to himself and become stronger, but he feared that one of the Nine had tried to take a hand against Alex, or one of the Rouge Four.

He kept much of the knowledge he had of magic and those he knew of who could use it to himself. Until now he had deemed the Nine's existence of no importance, confident they would ignore his actions. It was most likely a strengthened Lasorian, or one of the other Rouge Four.

What played on Zanier's mind was Alex's show. When had he learned that? And what was it exactly? Having no way to sense it, he had to judge the strength of the attacks from the reaction of demonic power that deflected it. It had been substantially stronger than anything Alex had thrown at them. That also raised the question about why Alex didn't ignore the demonic shields. Was there something about demonic magic that could stop Alex from ignoring it?

"Zanier," Kyle said.

"Yes?"

"I think we should attack tomorrow during the day"

"So soon?"

"We have to assume that Alex is at least somewhat fatigued. By morning, most of us will be back in top shape—plus Alex seems to be stronger at night. We have to hit him while he's weak—especially after what he showed us tonight. Those lightning bolts were from him. From what I know about offensive magic, I'd say they pack a punch. I fear Alex was just toying with us tonight," Zanier said.

"Ready the mages at dawn. We'll attack just before noon."

"Yes, sir."

CHAPTER 19

Molly's steady breath warmed Alex's neck. She snuggled up against him with her arms around his neck. The previous night was a blur of images that stopped being solid when he had fallen on the street. Alex remembered cursing Lasorian and thinking he was going to kill Molly. He remembered eleven voices in his head. The number made sense to him; he had heard eleven different voices, some more dominant than others were. He had also felt them touch the shadow through him as if they were one near-perfect entity. He had felt the darkness flinch at their touch and obey them without struggle—even in the massive amounts they required. It fought him at every turn when he tried something big. He hadn't seen what they had done or how they had done it—he just felt their darkness. His awareness of everything was gone now, but he didn't regret it. His psychotic laughing and ranting made him angry. Molly stirred at his side and she smiled when their eyes met.

"They're brown again. I like you better like this—you're not so scary." Alex frowned at her, and she giggled and snuggled closer. She put an arm around him and rested her head on his chest. "Don't wake me up for another hour or two. You need to sleep too."

Alex couldn't help himself as he began stroking Molly's hair.

She said, "Good. I like this better too."

"Molly, I can't stay."

He sat up and rubbed the side of his cheek. Molly groaned as she rolled away. Touching his face again, he realized it was burned. "What was that for?"

"Why don't go have your pretty little mage girl heal it? Oh, right—they don't like you. Perhaps in fighting them, one will be nice enough to deal with that burn."

Alex stared at her in amazement. "Molly, if I'm not there to stop them, no one else will."

"Yeah, go ahead and get yourself killed. It's only during the day—or do you think I don't know how your powers work by now? At night, you have basically an infinite supply of power, but during the day, you're pretty much just a beefed-up mage."

"I can draw power from any shadow—and there's plenty in the city."

"Enough to hold back an army of mages? Or are you going to do that wall thing again, which I'm sure you can't do during the day."

"I can do enough."

"Enough! What you can do is get yourself killed!"

Alex frowned as he strode toward the bathroom. "This time, don't come with me. I can't keep you safe all the time."

"Safe?" Molly held up her palms and each one ignited. "I'm a warlock now—well, witch, in case you haven't noticed—and can take damn well care of myself!"

Alex smiled at her as he walked into the shadow of the bathroom door. The awareness came back, but it was weak compared to the other night. Whatever had happened the night before had left at least some mark on him. *This could be useful.* Alex reached out toward the shadow and went to teleport. He felt resistance like the time Lasorian had stopped him, except now he was confident that it would not take much effort to shatter the resistance. Letting out a small wave of darkness, he felt Molly's concentration.

Her hands shaped weird signs and she was staring at him, gathering darkness; Alex teleported from the shadow of the door to the shadow of the bed. He shattered Molly's spell. She gasped and her hands dropped to her side. Her eyes glazed for a second, and Alex reached out to steady her. When he touched her shoulder, she flinched away.

"Why did you try to stop me?"

"You're going to get hurt!"

"Molly, I'll be fine. Are you okay? I didn't know it would hurt you."

Alex's pulse quickened when he looked her over. He hadn't really looked at her since she had bonded the succubus, but now that he did, it was all he could do to look away. If she was beautiful before, she was gorgeous now. Her hair was much redder than it had been before. Even sleep-ruffled, it looked exotic. Her eyes were larger and a bit of deep red added to her beauty. Her lips were slightly fuller and redder. Her shoulders seemed smoother and more elegant. Her breasts seemed fuller—if that was possible—and some was visible from the top of her loose top. Her waist was smoother and her hips were rounder. Her jeans clung to her long legs.

Alex redirected his eyes to hers when he realized that he was staring. She was smiling. *Oh God, she is beautiful.* Alex breathed in and instantly his heart started beating faster. He wanted kiss her—those smiling lips were amazing.

"See something, Alex? I thought you might have noticed by now." Her voice was smoldering. Alex hadn't felt this way since—had he ever felt this way? Alex thought he remembered, but he couldn't think clearly. All he wanted to do was hold Molly, kiss her, and make love to her. *That thought wasn't me.*

Alex tried to speak, but he choked on the words when Molly brushed the hair away from his face. Alex hadn't felt himself lean forward, but Molly wasn't tall enough to reach his lips if he hadn't. They were kissing and Alex couldn't think any longer. Molly was in his arms and they fell onto the bed. Her clothes didn't come off quickly enough so he reached out with his power and tore them from her. She had the same problem with his jumpsuit. Heat rippled around Alex's body as he kissed her mouth and tasted its sweetness. Alex felt guided by an unseen force as they made love. The pleasure from her body was exhilarating.

Neither of them had released control of their powers; darkness and fire danced around the room. Intertwined as their masters were, the sheets had caught fire, but neither of them noticed. Alex watched as sweat rolled down Molly's neck and between her breasts. Time seemed to dissipate and nothing mattered but her touch. He had no idea how long they made love. Exhausted, Alex fell asleep with Molly in his arms.

※   ※   ※

A group of mages walked down a Tampa street as if they ran the place. In theory they did, but chances were it wasn't that group of mages. They were all the same, walking around in their green robes and expecting everyone to get out of their way. Zanier had left a bunch behind when he moved north with his army of mercenaries and mages. Will had learned that most of those who were left behind were either weak or untrained. He had been disgusted by how the majority of mages treated their nongifted peers like they were less than human.

Will had also discovered that the majority of mages that were left behind could hardly create a shield. Simon had found that out when he accidently angered a younger one. He had thrown two knives after he saw how much effort it took to stop Simon's knife strikes before he shot a dull white light at Simon. He only suffered a minor burn and a headache from hitting a wall. The second of Will's knives had found a home in the young man's shoulder.

Will had heard very little of anyone doing anything against the mages—even though the vastly more powerful and well-trained ones had gone north. The mages had done a pretty solid job in beginning to clean up the city, which had been a dump before they had gotten there. Even though bigger gangs still ran, they were waiting to see what the mages did before they tried anything. The recruiting of mages had also put a damper on the opposition because almost everyone knew someone who knew someone in some way who'd joined the mages—if they didn't know someone themselves.

All and all, things were pretty uneventful in Tampa since the mages arrived. Mike and Will walked down the downtown streets. Simon had left not too long ago, saying he needed to go get something. Will didn't care; he and Mike probably wouldn't find the guy they were looking for. The Red Brothers Gang was the largest in Tampa. Will didn't understand it a hundred percent, but Mike and Simon said they needed to contact someone who knew what was going on in more than just the immediate area. They needed to know where the mages had gone. With the TV stations in the area now controlled by the mages, Simon didn't trust them. Will didn't think there was much not to trust on the TVs. Other than the weatherman, there was nothing else on besides old TV shows that Will could watch when he flipped through the channels in a diner or store.

Will hardly noticed when Mike led them off the main road and down an alley. Will almost walked right into Mike's back when he stopped before a large black man.

"Oh," Will said when he suddenly saw knives flash into Mike's hand. The large man had dreads and a goatee. He easily threw Mike against the side of a brick building. Seeing Mike's knives, he drew a pistol out of his pants and aimed at Mike. Will had gotten his knives into his hands before the man could make use of the gun. Will threw a knife into the man's wrist, causing him to drop the weapon. The man reached into his pants again, but this time Mike moved and blocked the potential route for Will's next knife. Mike suddenly dropped his knife and spread his hands. Will sidestepped Mike for a clear angle and saw the man had yet another gun drawn in his left hand.

"Drop the knife, boy. I will kill your friend before you get that knife in me."

Will knew that was true, but he also knew that he'd get a knife in the man. "Drop the gun."

The man smirked before lowering his gun and pushing Mike away. Tucking the gun back into his pants, he pulled a cloth from a pocket and began wrapping his wrist. Will relaxed his arm, but still held onto the knife.

"How old are you, boy?"

"Thirteen." The man laughed. Mike backed away and put his knife away. "How do you have so many guns?"

"The Reds buy from Smith and Wesson—we get what the New Americans don't have them pumping out."

"How? We're down from the Boston area. I'm from Western Mass—not far from Springfield. I've never heard of them selling to anyone but the government anymore."

"We have a section up there whose leader is friendly with one of their heads. How old are you? Eighteen? Come with me. I need to get this sewed up."

"Do you have a name?" Will asked.

"You?"

"Will Emerson."

"Dante Smith."

Mike shook his head. "Let's go."

Will continued. "What was earlier for?"

Dante smiled and said, "Ever been in a gang, boy?"

"No."

Dante laughed. "Think I can find a place for you."

Chapter 20

Alex felt cold as he paced across the top of a building in the middle of Savannah. Zanier's army had taken position and would move soon—all of it this time. He had no way to prevent it. Molly's voice rang in his head, reminding him that he was not nearly as powerful now as he was at night. The sun was high in the sky. Zanier had probably figured out how he was so strong and would not move till Alex was as weak as possible.

Alex reached out for power and kicked his foot against the roof. He felt weak and felt an intense yearning for something he couldn't have. His heart was pounding as he settled himself against the railing along the roof. Patting his side, he felt the blade. He had not brought it with him the other night. Molly had pretty much stabbed him with it trying to get him to take it with him.

He spent several hours in Molly's arms. He was pretty sure that she had faked sleeping as long as possible to keep him there—and he loved her for it. The thought stung him almost as hard as when he realized that it was true. When he was younger, he always thought that it would be wonderful to love someone. What Alex felt was a sorrow so consuming that he felt like giving up and never moving again. He felt that he was betraying Hannah—whom he felt no less for. He felt that having feelings for either of them was betraying the other. The mages massed together, and Alex wondered if Hannah was in there.

If Molly felt the same way toward him, he couldn't go back. He had to get away from her so that she wouldn't follow him anymore. He hated the idea of separating himself from her but he feared her getting hurt even more. He would have to fight and he had seen how hurt Molly was every time that she watched him go. He knew he would only cause her pain so he had to leave her.

He'd thought on what Hannah had said about him not having a cause, only fighting to get in the way of others. He knew what his cause was now. The voices from the night before had confirmed it. He was going to end this war, not just in America but everywhere. He'd change the world, that's what shadow casters did.

He hadn't figured out what to do about Hannah yet. Almost on cue, Alex felt heat on his back and the faint feel of demonic magic over the stronger feel of arcane magic. He turned around and saw Lasorian and Molly.

"I didn't do anything to make her come, Alex. She taught herself a way to track you down."

Lasorian brushed some dirt from the side of high-necked dark robes that opened in the front at the legs to reveal loose-fitting black trousers and high black leather boots. Molly was wearing the same thing. The robes moved unnaturally and seemed clingy despite the wind. Alex caught himself as he examined Molly.

"What are you wearing?"

"She wanted me to get her something that—"

"I could wear fighting. It's not bulletproof, but it has other things that are helpful. When witches and warlocks fight, they wear robes like these."

Alex turned away from Molly. "You are leaving; I don't want you here."

"I don't care." Alex heard a step forward. "I'm here and I'm going to help!"

Ignoring her, Alex said to Lasorian, "Why are you here?"

Lasorian walked away from Molly. "I'm here because I want to watch as this happens."

"You watch a lot," Alex said coldly. "Whose side are you on?"

"Side? My side, of course. Right now, watching this helps me." Lasorian laughed slightly and Molly looked coldly toward Lasorian. "I'm here to watch—your girlfriend seems to think I'm here to fight."

"Why else would you come—I was here last night."

"And you helped."

"Not in the battle."

"Alex was going to die and you helped him!"

"I thought it would have been wasteful for him to die that way."

"You don't want him to die; you'll step in if it goes that far."

Alex watched Zanier's army begin to move and—judging from the end of their argument—Lasorian and Molly had seen the army's movement too. Alex reached out to the darkness and teleported to the ground into the shadow of another building. Alex pulled darkness into him as he sprinted down the city. Refugees from the city were now safely north of the city. No one was there to watch shadows being pulled toward the figure sprinting down the roads. Zanier's army had split into several smaller groups that entered the city from different locations. Alex, trying to conserve power, was out of breath by the time he came upon the first group. Soldiers dropped to cover and opened fire while mages stood and attacked Alex. He felt his shield struggle under the force of an attack that he would have laughed at the night before. Ducking around a corner for a second, he gathered himself before he lifted into the air and whipped around the corner. Flying higher, he sent a shower of shadowy darts down onto the mage's shield. Alex watched mages drop as he left them behind. He found another group before they saw him and launched the same attack. About to move on, Alex felt a massive explosion which sent him to the ground. His shield held as he hit. Rising quickly to his feet, he called power toward him as Tantalus charged at him.

Alex dove and ducked around fireballs as Tantalus did the same for Alex's attacks. Alex knew that the duel was in his favor—all he needed to do was hit Tantalus once. If Alex sensed right, Tantalus didn't even have a shield up. Tantalus constantly moved closer. Alex was astonished that the old man could move this well as a fireball slammed into his shield.

Tantalus was on him. Swords of pure fire appeared in each of his hands. They slammed into Alex's shield with tremendous force. Drawing the long knife, they danced. Alex wasn't used to fighting with weapons like this, but he caught on quickly. He was surprised that when his blade and Tantalus' fire swords hit, they stopped each other. It wasn't a metal-to-metal clink that he heard, but more of a hot-pan-hitting-cold-water noise. His blade suddenly heated up. Alex quickly drew out the heat—an easy task taking up little power compared to his shield being struck. Tantalus had his two flaming weapons and Alex had his long knife in his right hand. He lobbed bolts at Tantalus from his left. Alex couldn't understand how Tantalus was so strong. He knew that he was enhancing himself with his power, but his skill was ridiculous. Tantalus got through to him and struck his shield repeatedly. Alex had seen and fought others who were quicker than Tantalus—even with his magic-fortified body. Alex was enhancing his own movements with the power he was drawing in to the point where he was actually faster. No matter where Alex attacked, he was there with a parry or avoided the attack all together. Alex knew he could outlast Tantalus, but he couldn't possibly drive back all of Zanier's army at this rate.

Alex stumbled as his shield was wrapped in lightning, followed by several blows from Tantalus. The lightning had come from Kyle. Alex figured that he was the only one in the second group that had showed up willing to attack him while he and Tantalus were in such close quarters. Tantalus lifted backward into the air, fire blades fading from his hands. Alex felt hell open up on him from two different directions as the remnants of Tantalus' group and Kyle's group opened up on him. It steadily grew brighter and brighter as Alex drew in power. With all the light around him, Alex could hardly see his enemies. Reaching out with both hands, he randomly launched bolts at both groups.

The majority of the attack ended, allowing Alex to get away from both groups. He found an alley and collapsed into it. Breathing heavily, Alex reached out to every shadow around him. Light seemed to bend as Alex gained strength. Everything became steadily brighter. Lightning bolts and fireballs tore into his shield when several mages saw him.

Lifting himself into the air, he felt even more attacks hit him.

Alex tried to move, but he slowly felt himself lower and his head burned. Closing his eyes, he tried to pull more power. He had never reached this deeply before during the day—it burned his head as he tried for more. He blindly shot bolts of shadows down on where he thought the mages were. He no longer tried to control what he was firing—random bolts in varying strengths rained into Savannah.

Opening his eyes, he saw only white. Something grabbed him as the burning in his head and the light that filled his vision took over all his awareness.

❋   ❋   ❋

Tantalus tried to cover his eyes, leaving the remainder of the assault to the other mages. The light was so intense that even shutting his eyelids provided little protection. Frankly he was disappointed. He had hoped for more out of Alex from what Alex had shown them on previous encounters. Tantalus doubted that Zanier even knew that he knew what a warlock was—or if he had even sensed what was beneath his demonic power. Tantalus prided himself on his magical and human senses. Magic had kept his human senses from deteriorating with age. It was his keen feel for magic that had let him feel the store inside that warlock. It was covered in an incredibly thick store of demonic power, but it was there—and there was a lot of it. Zanier and Kyle both lacked that sensitivity. Tantalus was quite sure that he was one of two with his senses. In all of the mages, he doubted that the boy would know what to look for. He was too busy staring at Hannah when he should have been training.

Tantalus jerked his hand away from his face, fireballs flaring to life in his hands. Two sources of power had appeared near where Alex should be. He recognized one right away as being the warlock from the previous night, and the other was significantly weaker and possessed only demonic power. He sent the fireballs at both sources. The stronger one's reaction was smooth and perfect as he deflected the fireball, but the weaker had a much slower reaction. It relied on a sustained shield that jerked full of power—way more than was necessary to deflect the fireball—as if it hadn't even felt or seen the fireball coming and had panicked when it hit.

Tantalus felt them long before he saw them. Many of the mages up front never saw what hit them as two massive golden fireballs tore through their ranks. Tantalus dove to the side as the fireball, near invisible in the blinding light, tore by before it used itself on the shield of the mage behind him.

A voice followed the fireballs "My name is Lasorian— Demon of Light." *Lasorian? Demon of Light?* "Once of the Circle—now of the Rogue Four." *Circle?* "And I do not deem it the hour of the shadow caster's death!"

A figure could be seen now clad all in black. The hood of his robes pulled over his head, his right hand was held palm up with an orb of light in his hand. The area around him seemed to return to normal light as he walked forward. The doom expanded drastically, containing Tantalus. Solid light surrounded him.

Tantalus saw Kyle step forward. Tantalus figured that he had joined the group after everything became so bright. He hadn't seen him earlier and he certainly had not used any magic after he had first encountered the duel. Tantalus narrowed his eyes at his superior war mage. He had always been jealous of the young man's impressive talent. Something had happened the other night between him and Sara. Tantalus aimed to find out what when this was through, which meant they had to deal with this warlock. With Kyle, he stood on his right.

"And what do you want with us?" Kyle said.

"My ultimate goal for this encounter is to ensure the shadow caster's survival."

"Take him and leave," Tantalus said sternly. The man was radiating power. From this close it was like standing next to an inferno. With Tantalus' senses, it was hard to appear calm. "We want the city—not the boy's life. Personally, I enjoy fighting him—he's surprisingly entertaining. When the rest of us merge, there will be several hundred mages here—including Zanier. You are strong, but surely you do not wish to fight all of us. Take Tantalus' advice—take Alex and leave." Lasorian could level the city if he felt like it. He wasn't sure about Kyle, but he was not about to commit suicide by trying to fight this man. It wasn't like fighting Alex. He had never seen Alex control his power with any type of finesse in any of their battles.

Lasorian said, "I guess logically that makes sense, but you obviously do not know what it is I was—and in a way, I still am."

"The Circle—or whatever it is you were talking about?" Kyle asked.

"Yes. How much has Zanier told you about them? I'm guessing not much." His voice suddenly strengthened so that all the nearby mages could hear. Tantalus felt magic being used for this—not demonic magic, but innate mage magic. He doubted that anyone else felt it. "How many of you even know what a warlock is?"

A hum came up from the surrounding mages as they asked each other what they knew. One shouted over the rest, "Warlocks are abominations who traffic with demons. They are the reason for the witch hunts that killed mages! That is what Zanier's histories say!"

Tantalus narrowed his eyes and took hold of his power, earning himself an amused look from Lasorian.

"For the most part, that is the truth. However, it was the failings of several—not of the whole—that led to the witch hunts. A warlock is a person that has studied the magic texts and learned how to create a circle from which that person binds a demon to their soul, gifting them with demonic powers. With study they learn to use this power in spells. The warlock's will is no different than you and your power—if not more complicated."

"And the Circle?" Kyle asked.

"Zanier has told you nothing?" Lasorian asked.

"What was there to tell, Lasorian?" All heads turned to watch Zanier step into the dome from the light. He was radiating enough power to cause Tantalus great discomfort, but he was a candle next to a campfire in comparison to Lasorian. "The Circle is no more and the Nine will do nothing once Alex is dealt with."

"The Circle was created before the formation of the Roman Empire—at the end of Greece's greatest strength on Sicily—to act as ruling and controlling force over those who use magic."

"The Roman Empire? Greece? How were they able to survive this long? How was magic forgotten like it was?" Kyle asked. "If they were able to keep getting new members and maintain themselves, then magic must not have been forgotten everywhere. Zanier, are their more magic users than us in the world?"

"I doubt it—unless any of the Circle have trained others in this time. Lasorian, we've met before and you look no older. I'd love to know how all thirteen original members have lived this long. You proved me right when you encountered me those years ago. Sara wasn't your immediate granddaughter. You had a lover once that the Circle wouldn't let you make like you. You've watched over your children's children and their children and all their children since then, haven't you? That is how I was able to get you to reveal yourself to me when I convinced Sara to join us. How much does she look like her? Not much can be done to force Lasorian into an act of violence."

Lasorian's gaze turned to ice, focusing on Zanier.

"Zanier, I wonder what deal you made with them—whose puppet you are." When Lasorian stepped forward, Kyle flinched, but Zanier's expression didn't change. Tantalus focused more closely on Zanier. "Or do you think you're acting independently? I wonder what the chances were of you coming across all those texts on magic that you possess."

"You are a fool, Lasorian—a fool whose has lived on this earth too long. I would hate to end your over several millennium of existence now. With so many questions unanswered, be careful whom you provoke." Zanier stepped closer to Lasorian. Tantalus examined Zanier closer. *Can he really not feel how powerful Lasorian is?* Tantalus again wondered at the exact strength of his gift. Did his sense really extend that much further than the other mages?

"Zanier, you are a talented mage, but you know terribly little next to me. I am immortal—as are all thirteen members of the Circle." The crowd of mages erupted in gasps and mumbles. "I have seen the use of magic in the prime of its existence. I know more of it than you could ever dream of—and you cannot touch me."

"But I have a trump card, Lasorian—one you know of as well as me. You won't touch me as long as she follows me."

Zanier smiled, yet Lasorian's composure did not change.

"You can't use Sara that way!"

Zanier and Lasorian were surprised by Kyle's outburst. Tantalus took a step away from Kyle and looked him over.

"This is interesting. What is my granddaughter to you? I don't believe I know your name."

"I am Kyle. I love Sara and I will protect her! Her and our ... and our child!"

Lasorian nodded and Tantalus smiled smugly while Zanier nearly came close to gasping.

"We will talk later. Leave now or we will force you to, Lasorian."

"I had hoped this could wait a while longer, but if you wish for a slaughter of your mages, go ahead throw them at me."

Tantalus braced himself for Zanier's command, taking control of his power. Zanier's voice was instantly drowned out by the sound of lightning bolts, fire bolts, and balls of raw power. Tantalus was surprised to see the blue fireballs fly from Zanier's hands.

Tantalus lost sight of Lasorian for a moment in the chaos of attacks. A tidal wave of golden fire tore into the front ranks of mages. Most could not stand the attack and were incinerated. Tantalus' grip on his power faltered as it slipped from his control. Cursing himself he grasped at it, it kept slipping away from him like water through an open hand. This was a novice thing to do. How come he couldn't take control of his power? It was there and still strong, but he just couldn't take hold of it. Tantalus expected to be toasted by Lasorian's next attack. He realized that no one was doing anything. They were all confused—except Lasorian and Zanier. Lasorian was making hand motions. Tantalus felt demonic power floating in the mass of mages.

"Lasorian, I believe you're sweating," Zanier said. Tantalus focused on Lasorian's face. Sure enough, beads of sweat were rolling down his face. "Why is it you have silenced several hundred mages when you could simply blast them away?"

Silenced? Was that what this is called? Lasorian was using demonic magic to prevent the mages from touching their power. Tantalus thought that was remarkable. He wondered whether he could do the same with his magic. If he could, the uses in combat were limitless. Tantalus was confused about why Lasorian had not struck back. They might as well be normal people dressed up in green robes—unless whatever Lasorian was doing was taking up to much effort.

"Can't speak either it seems. What are you planning?" Zanier asked.

Tantalus touched his power and a fireball shot at Lasorian. Several others followed and the fireballs' direction shifted angling off in the light.

Lasorian smiled as an archway of fire formed.

"My job here is done." The archway slid over him and vanished with Lasorian. Tantalus felt his power being pulled by a will not his own.

❋   ❋   ❋

Hannah saw Molly carrying Alex. She seemed to have been struggling and was barely able to fly across the gaps on rooftops. The blinding light made it difficult, but she caught up to them. Molly had managed to make it to the river and was now sitting at the base of a tree. Alex's body was mostly in Molly's lap and his head was resting on her breasts. He showed no signs of consciousness.

She glared at Molly and asked, "Is he okay?"

"Alive, yes." Molly stroked his hair. Hannah noticed how it had gotten longer. "What did you say to him last night? He lost control and almost died. He was so exhausted when he left. I tried to stop him." Hannah knelt and touched the side of Alex's face—half to touch him, half to make sure that she could feel life. "I only made it worse."

"What happened? Last night we saw a battle. What do mean *he lost control*?"

"He was taken over by the previous shadow casters. They fought Lasorian through him."

"What? How?"

"I don't know. I just know they left him a mess. He was only half sane when I got him to fall asleep last night. He shouldn't have come. I tried everything. Oh my God, I can't believe I actually did it. I can't believe it. He was so weak, so I tried—he needs to eat."

"What did you do?" Hannah asked Molly.

"I . . . I . . . I seduced him. I mean—I used the ability. I bound a succubus."

"A succubus? You seduced him! What did you do?"

"We had sex."

"You had what?"

"In the residue from the magic—and the actual thing— we never released control of our powers. The room was a mess. I was exhausted and I wasn't even the subject of the seduction." She stroked his hair out of his face again.

Hannah was in shock. This girl had used demonic magic to have sex with Alex. She wanted to kill her right now. Knowing that she was strong enough to kill her, she touched her power.

Molly said, "I can feel you touching your power. Go ahead kill me if you want, but why don't you try to help Alex with it instead? I tried, but healing isn't something I can really do well."

Hannah had been about to blow Molly out of existence but Alex needed healing. She touched Alex's head and probed him. He was deathly tired. Ignoring the fatigue, he had absolutely no nutrition in his system. He must have not eaten a thing in weeks. *How is he still alive?* His back was riddled with poorly healed ribs and a bruised kidney. Half the muscles in his body had some sort of strain from overexertion. Hannah healed them and stopped probing. Hannah gasped when she couldn't stop the flow of power into Alex.

"What's wrong?" Molly asked.

"I healed him, but he's ... I can't stop my power from flowing into him. I think ... it's like ... I think he's pulling my power into him."

"How?"

"I don't know."

CHAPTER 21

The light seemed to have shades to it, but it still burned Alex's eyes. He could see shapes of men surrounding him. They were hunched over on their knees in apparent agony. Alex could hear their moans of pain and was sure that he was moaning too.

The odd light stretched endlessly in every direction. He realized that the men were clad in white and had hoods drawn up over their faces. He knew these men. He had heard their voices inside his head the night before. He wished he could do more to speak with them, but the pain was too much. Alex felt every weakness in his body amplified to the point where he was crippled. The thoughts he had—beside pain—were whether he was still alive and, if not, why death was so painful.

Something touched him, and a familiar presence soothed some of his pain.

"Hannah," he whispered, but his pain continued. One of the men had stopped writhing. He looked up at Alex, his face became visible, and it was very tan. He looked Arab. His face looked like it had seen much suffering.

Alex couldn't see anything travel between them, but he felt knowledge enter him and knew what to do. If he could feel a mage's power, he could take it as his own. Hannah's power was still inside him. Alex grasped at it, pulling it into him. The relief was small at first, but welcome. He felt Hannah's power deplete, but was still desperate for more. Only slightly renewed, he stretched out for more and found it. He was like a man dying of thirst finding a lake of fresh water.

Alex started with the power they were releasing and pulled it toward him. The light around him took most of it, but enough power still reached him. Alex opened his eyes and Molly gasped. He lifted himself from her lap, still focusing on the power of the mages.

"Alex!" Molly grabbed at his arm. "Alex, your eyes are blue again."

He saw Hannah lying on the ground, barely able to lift her head.

"Alex?" she said softly.

He focused on the power and lifted his right hand. A shadow appeared around it, the light lost its intensity, and a flow of pale blue light flowed into his hand. The light returned to normal and he felt the amount of power he was absorbing increase drastically. He laughed slightly at the ecstasy. He watched hundreds of mages appear from around the buildings. The light was radiating off them. They launched attacks at him, but he didn't even raise a shield. An aura of shadow surrounded him and the attacks began to orbit around him before he consumed them.

He became the center of a light show. Fire and lightning of varying colors surrounded him as they were consumed by darkness. Blue light flowed from the mages into Alex. The power he was feeling surpassed anything he had ever felt before—an army of mages and their power were his. Alex laughed madly as he became stronger.

"Alex, what are you doing?" Molly's voice passed through his consciousness like a whisper. What was she compared to this?

"Power."

"Alex!" said Zanier.

"Quiet, mage—your power is mine!"

"Is it Alex I'm talking to—or the shadow?"

"I am the shadow caster—you are nothing before me!"

"You are going mad," Zanier said. "How does it feel to have so much power?" His strengthening had slowed. The light now only came from Zanier. "You even took her power. Look at her—she is too weak to move because of you."

Alex tore the remainder of Zanier's power from him, leaving him to stumble and fall to his knees. Alex laughed as he struggled to stay on his hands and knees.

"What now, Zanier? The mage finally sees where he actually belongs—on his knees before the shadow caster—like hundreds of mages before you."

"Alex, what are you talking about?" Molly's voice was trembling.

What did she mean? Alex could clearly remember hundreds of mages surrendering their power to him at the beginning of every day. With it, he leveled all armies that stood before him. *Wait, when did I do that?* The memories seemed so real.

An impact on the side of his head knocked him off his feet. He rolled across the ground. Crawling to his knees, he raised a shield as more impacts followed the first, slamming harmlessly against his shield. Alex saw pebbles, dirt, and dust rising around him. Soldiers had positioned themselves on buildings or other sources of cover all around him. Alex's hands surged with darkness. Bolts of darkness shot from his hands at the soldiers. Moving at breakneck speed, Alex flew to the rear of the soldiers' positions. Bolts of darkness flowed from his hands and slaughtered the mercenaries. Blasts slammed into his shield and temporary blinded him in the fire and smoke.

When the smoke cleared, Alex saw more mercenaries. They had come out of the buildings and were shooting at him. Alex laughed at how pitiful they were to fight him, but he realized that not all of them were shooting at him. Molly was backing toward the river and struggling to keep them off. Hannah was also trying to get out of the line of fire, but she was weak and unable to defend herself. He flew to the closest shadow before teleporting to the shadow of the tree nearest Molly. He erected a barrier between them and the mercenaries.

Alex lifted Hannah off the ground.

"Alex, your eyes are back!" Molly exclaimed.

"My eyes?"

"It doesn't matter." Her eyes were very bright. Alex felt faint. "What was that?"

"What?"

"You just went hazy like you were half there."

Alex grabbed her hand and brought her into the shadow of the tree. "I didn't do anything."

Alex teleported to the top of a nearby building. As he landed, his vision went blurry and he saw the clearing in the woods where he had met Lasorian.

"Alex, you just did it again—only it was longer."

"I'm fine."

Alex teleported back to where the mercenaries were. He sent attacks at the mercenaries—enough to knock them out, but not kill them. The power was incredible, but the memories of another person disappeared—though some he could still recall. Alex gathered a large sum of power before his vision went hazy again. This time he was in his and Molly's room. He had time to feel the ground before he was torn back to Savannah. The large sum of power slipped from his control as he fell to his knees in front of the horde of powerless mages. They had gathered and were retreating behind the mercenaries who were organizing the retreat. Alex wrapped power around all of them, but it slipped from his hands again as his head went hazy—this time it was rapid visions before he landed by the river.

The sun had gone low and the shadows stretched longer. Alex tried to stand, but his head went hazy again and he was thrown from random place to random place till he focused on the shadow of the tree. Landing on his feet this time, he saw Molly running toward him.

"Alex!" she cried as the grabbed him.

"Molly." Alex focused as hard he could. So much of his power was out of his control. He felt himself being pulled in a hundred different directions.

"Alex, what's happening to you?"

"I can't control it."

"Please, you have to stay with me."

"I ... I want to." Alex felt himself torn violently. It was all he could do to resist it.

She held onto him so tightly that it was hard to breathe. Alex mournfully watched the sunset as his incredible store of power reached for the coming night. "Did you get Hannah to safety?"

"She's with the mages. They are leaving the city for now, but the mercenaries are securing it."

"Molly?"

"What?"

"I don't know what's going to happen when the sun sets."

"You're staying here—that's what's going to happen." Alex smiled as he stroked her hair. He could control the violent pulls now even though they came more often. He knew that once there was more power to draw on, he'd lose control.

"I'm sorry for everything. I'm sorry that it'll hurt you when I'm gone."

"Alex, shut up! What are you talking about? Don't be sorry for anything—you've done nothing to apologize for."

"I took you away from your family and your life. In return, I gave you this world and all this fighting."

"Alex, meeting you was greatest thing that ever happened to me. I love you!" Alex's heart felt as if it had suddenly become lead. Unable to speak, he watched the sun pass below the trees.

The pulls on him suddenly became more violent. Alex knew it wouldn't be long. Pulling away from Molly for a moment, he kissed her. Her mouth tasted so sweet and never had he been kissed so passionately. Using this moment as a distraction, he drew on what power he could control—binding Molly to where she was and tying it through him so she couldn't try anything. She realized what he had done.

"Alex!"

He smiled as he stepped away from her.

"Good-bye, Molly."

Tears dripped down her face. Alex resisted as long as he could, but as daylight faded, there was too much power to resist.

Alex was torn from where he stood. The knot of tied power tore, adding more to the chaos of his power. Alex didn't recognize where he ended up—a thousand feet in the air over a city, to an alleyway, a forest. He lost track and his stomach was ready to empty itself—if there was anything to empty. He felt an awful nausea with an intense headache. Alex was submerged underwater. Opening his mouth, he tasted saltwater before being torn from there. Alex felt rocks under his feet and was suddenly chilled as he saw snow around him before he teleported again.

Hitting sand, he fell on his face. There was nothing left to him. He couldn't feel his power anymore—or any of the darkness around him. He coughed out sand as he saw a ghost-like figure standing before him. It was the same man he had seen before in the light—only he was in black and translucent.

"Sleep well, my son. You will not die yet—no, not yet."

Alex lost consciousness with those words in his head.

EPIL⊕GUE

Nine figures in black robes stood in a circle inside a large, domed room with a thirteen-point star elegantly carved into the ground. At the end of each point was a circle. A larger circle in the middle held a massive, glowing red ruby. The nine figures stood in a circle with four empty circles remaining.

"So it has begun," a feminine voice said from under a black hood. She stood next to an empty circle to her left.

"Yes, Floriana, it would seem that way," said the tall man next to her.

"The shadow caster has vanished," said a masculine voice from a shorter figure. "Marius, have you succeeded?"

"Yes, Vitus. You may come in now, dear."

A slender male figure gestured and a girl with dark brown hair and brown eyes walked into the room. She was wearing white trousers and a loose white shirt. She was quite pretty, but her eyes were unfocused and she moved mindlessly— never looking away from right in front of her.

"Marius, do you ever consider not draining your subjects completely of personality? It would be nice to have at least one with mind enough to look frightened once in a while," a sultry female voice complained.

"It is not Marius' job to entertain your odd fancies, Quintina."

"Oh, Julius, you speak of odd fancies. I don't believe they call you Decimator of Nations for no reason."

"Quiet—all of you," boomed a deep voice.

"Oh, is Brutus irritated," the voice from before said.

"Cecialia, don't push him. Let us begin," the tall man said.

"Yes, Cyprianais," said Cecialia.

"Marius, are we ready?" said Cyprianais.

"Yes, yes, we are," Marius answered.

"Then let us begin."

In unison, the nine robed figures began chanting. The ruby increased in brilliance while the girl in white stood emotionlessly inside the circle at the middle of the star. A narrow torrent of fire erupted from the ruby, but the girl still didn't move. The torrent of fire took shape, becoming a naked feminine figure with four arms. It had pale skin and long black horns. In one arm, it held a bow and, in two others, it held swords.

"So I am summoned once again. Couldn't you have found a different demon to do your bidding?"

"Oh, Sativa. What other demon could we trust to hunt down the shadow caster?"

"Cyprianais, you were always a stickler for consistency. It was Lasorian that could truly be innovative and I see that those four have yet to return."

"Silence, demon—or do you want to make this harder on you?"

The demon laughed and said, "Oh, Cyprianais. I submit to your will. I assume this is to be my body this time. What relation is she to the shadow caster?"

"She is his half sister," Marius answered.

"Marius, you always struck to close too the heart. I can't wait for his reaction when he realizes what you did to his sister," the demon said.

"He doesn't know she exists," Marius answered.

"Ah, too bad. I might have to do something about that."

"Sativa, your command is to track down the shadow caster. His name is Alexander Montague Savadora. If you can avoid killing him, we'd like a chance to speak with him."

Cyprianais signaled for the ritual to continue. The demon nodded and all nine figures chanted in unison. The demon shut her eyes and glowed red before she dissipated into a red fog. The rest continued the chant while Marius lifted his hands into the air and started performing hand symbols while he chanted something different. The fog swirled into a long thin line. The girl appeared to inhale and the line of red fog went into the girl's mouth.

The girl's back arched as she was lifted into the air. She floated to the middle of the circle and a beam of red light from the ruby hit her. She spasmed and seemed to glow. Marius rejoined the rest with the chant. Cyprianais stopped chanting, held his palms in the air, and roared. His hands ignited in white fire and a ring of white rose from the outside of the circle. He roared again and the fire and the ring of light faded. The chanting ceased as the girl crouched down. She tensed and breathed deeply before standing. Reaching out her arms, she flexed each muscle and finger. She followed this by jumping from one foot to the other. The girl performed a back somersault out of the circle.

"Sativa, how does the real world feel?" Cyprianais asked smugly.

"It's good to breathe again."

"Can you feel him?" asked Brutus.

Sativa closed her eyes for a moment before opening them.

"He's the cold feeling, right? He is to the southeast. I believe you called that the Middle East."

"Well, then, you should begin hunting immediately," Floriana said.